Heart Conditions
Sentimental Adventures in Turn-of-the-Century Italy

Matilde Serao

Kazabo Publishing

Table of Contents

FOREWORD

Matilde Serao was born in Greece in 1856 to an Italian father and a Greek mother. Her father had moved to Greece for political reasons, but in 1860 the family returned to Naples, where he began work as a journalist. Matilde, who spent her youth in a family with constant financial difficulties, absorbed the atmosphere of the newspaper as a child and overcame her financial straits by devoting herself to a life of constant, disciplined writing. She was very prolific, and was nominated for the Nobel Prize in Literature on six occasions.

Her first books reveal the strong influence of the *Verismo* movement. Her realism deals with the psychological and pathological analysis of her characters, the same approach that we find in Luigi Capuana's work. Later, however, she wrote more romantic – even Gothic – novels and short stories. She was always, first and foremost, a professional writer, adapting herself to the shifting tastes of her public.

At twenty-six, she moved from Naples to Rome where she met her husband, Edoardo Scarfoglio. Together, they founded *Il Corriere di Roma*, the first Italian attempt to reproduce a daily newspaper similar to those of the Parisian press of the day. When the couple moved back to Naples, Matilde edited *Il Corriere di Napoli*. In 1892 she co-founded *Il Mattino* with her husband, which became the most important daily paper in southern Italy. Finally, after separating from her husband, she established and ran her own newspaper, "*Il Giorno*" in 1904 and continued to do so until her death in 1927.

Through her literary efforts, Serao was able to carve a place for herself in disciplines largely dominated by men. In Italy, she became known for her eccentricity and determination, for her aggressive and magnetic personality capable of establishing her authority anywhere. She was just as comfortable in the offices of male-dominated newspapers as she was in the literary salons of the time. She was also well-known and admired in France, and was, in turn, influenced by the French literary tradition. It was in Paris, in one of the famous literary salons of the time, that she met Edith Wharton, who was intrigued by the Neapolitan's acute intelligence and eccentric appearance, in striking contrast with the fashionable ladies of the literary salons of the French capital. Wrote Wharton, "With her strident dress and intonation, she seemed an incongruous figure in that drawing-room where everything was in half-shades and semi-tones, but when she began to speak we had found our master… Her training as a journalist had given her a rough-and-ready knowledge of life, and an experience of public affairs, totally lacking in the drawing-room Corinnes whom she outrivaled in wit and eloquence."

Despite her successes, Serao always ostensibly

espoused a strongly anti-feminist position because she had great doubts – despite her own example – that the feminism of the time could bring about lasting social change. She remained convinced that passion is the prime driver of social affairs. "It will never be possible to convince a woman's heart that love isn't the most important event in her life… Feminism will never find anything as important as love to fill a woman's life…" she declared.

In this collection, we explore Matilde Serao's views of love and relationships through her short stories. These stories make it clear that Serao was not a sort of Italian Barbara Cartland. Many of her stories are firmly rooted in the *Verismo* movement and examine love and relationships as they are in the real world rather than how they might be imagined in a perfect one. But in the context of her time, all of her stories are deeply transgressive. Late nineteenth and early twentieth century Italy – the time and place where Serao wrote – had very strong societal norms regarding love and marriage. Each of Serao's stories has a twist, a sting in the tail, that sometimes subtly, sometimes openly, subverts those norms with originality, elegance and irony.

It is almost as if, while acknowledging the primacy of love and relationships, she is a bit sorry about it. These stories do not so much celebrate romantic love as hold it up to a magnifying glass, and often a very uncomfortable magnifying glass, at that.

Matilde Serao's anti-feminist statements are a matter of record. Yet it is hard to square them with the totality of her life and work, as this collection shows. Her apparent disdain may come from the perceived failure of other early-twentieth-century Italian women to live up to her almost-impossibly high example of independence and self-determination. Perhaps Serao was not so much an anti-feminist as a feminist ahead of her time.

Chiara Giacobbe

The stories that we have chosen and translated for this publication – appearing here for the first time in English – are taken from three different collections: Raccolta minima *(published in 1881),* Fior di passione *(published in 1899) and* La moglie di un grand'uomo ed altre novelle scelte dall'autrice *(published in 1919).*

IN A SMALL TOWN

Two rival families were recreating, in miniature, the feud between Capulets and Montagues: Only because they had regard for modern civilization, instead of shedding blood, they shed and spread money. Instead of dead people, there had been many very long and complicated trials; they quarreled for the sake of fighting, spite, and anger; they quarreled with that obstinate pleasure of suing that is one of the joys of the small towns. As usual, the quarrels were about silly things: A bit of water that went in the wrong direction; a lively goat that had jumped from the field of one to the field of the other; some stupid potatoes that, growing underground, had violated a border. All the piles of legal papers were raining down, and court clerks struggled, writing in their obscure style that was the last remembrance of the barbaric invasions, judgments were multiplying, trials got more and more confusing, the two lawyers were rubbing their hands for joy, and from the look of things, were sure to pass on to their children those lawsuits, as a precious inheritance. How that enmity between the Pasqualis and the Dericcas had started, no one knew exactly; on both sides, the explanations varied, but the one sure thing was a deep and declared hatred. Being neighbors in town, and having neighboring lands in the countryside, they often met, looking at each other with hostility; the women went to Mass in two different churches; if the Dericca girls wore blue dresses, the Pasquali girls immediately dressed in pink; at the meetings of the Municipal Council, the Pasqualis always had conservative opinions, and the Dericcas, of course, always progressive; what the one did, the other would not have done for all the money in the world; where the one went, the other would never show up. And then came gossip, slander, malicious whispering, greed of scandals, spiteful acts; in short, that kind of enjoyment that goes on in the small towns between two rival families. For this reason Carlo, the firstborn of the Pasqualis, and Maria, the second-born of the Dericcas, had the bright idea of falling in love.

The loves of small towns don't have much variety. They are mostly relationships that begin in childhood. They grow during games of hide-and-seek, and usually manifest themselves at family dances, continue in the gatherings where bingo is played, and always have their completion in front of the parish priest and the mayor. They are well-known loves—watched, agreed upon, recorded in the comings and goings from one house to the other; protected by grumpy grandparents, by priest uncles; they are known throughout the city; loves with no anxieties, no tears, no excessive tenderness, no fancies. Something very calm, very slow, the crystallization of love.

Carlo Pasquali, however, had had the incomparable luck to spend, one time, fifteen days in Naples, which made him look contemptuously at the provincial customs of the small towns; and Maria Dericca, in the dark of the night, had wept for the unfortunate heroines created by the famous romance novelist Mastriani and envied them their fantastic passions. Therefore, those two needed an exceptional love. It was, at first, a furtive glimpse, a word murmured in a whisper, and yet understood with a singular perception from the one who was destined to hear it; a carnation dropped from a balcony, surely due to the wind; a subtle pallor of his, a subtle blush of hers; then, through the intervention of a mischievous fifteen-year-old girl who used to iron in Maria's home, there was a note, a short answer; then a brief letter, a long letter, and finally the volumes of eight or ten sheets of paper that mark the highest point of love madness.

Alas! The joys of the two youths were short, and sudden was the pain that came to make them vanish. They were seen, spied, and the news reached their respective fathers, and all the thunders of the paternal wrath, made all the more bitter by eleven lawsuits, fell on the head of the poor lovers. Their balconies were closed; a lock appeared on the terrace door; each carnation on the plant was counted; walks were forbidden, or at least granted without previous announcement; the schedule of the Mass was changed every Sunday; but those two continued to love each other. The scoldings, the preachings, the prohibitions, and the difficulties did nothing but increase their love. During the night, in the winter, Maria got up, dressed, wrapped herself in a shawl and still in her slippers, holding her breath, trembling with fear, went down the stairs, to a window on the ground floor; her friend was in the street, leaning against the wall. So they used to talk for two or three hours, not minding the cold, the rain and the lost sleep; they talked without seeing each other, falling silent at each passer-by, cautiously restarting their conversation with the constant fear that Maria's relatives would wake up and find her talking to him. But what did they care about all this? They had in their hearts the light, the sun, the spring, the courage, the enthusiasm; the king could come, and they would not move. Instead, it was Maria's brother who arrived. One night he could not sleep, got up, and found her bedroom door ajar; he went down the stairs, heard a whisper, and caught his sister in the act. Without ceremony, he slammed the shutters in Carlo's face, slapped Maria, and brought her back to her room. The following morning, the little window on the ground floor was walled up, too bad if the staircase, as a result, remained somewhat dark.

Oh you, faithful lovers, who find yourselves suffering for an opposed love, imagine the despair of those two! Their letters could no longer be read, because their tears erased the words; lines of exclamation marks looked like Prussian soldiers, followed their daily appalling curses to fate, destiny, and other impersonal beings that could not be affected; thousands of fantastic projects were imagined, discussed, and then rejected. Carlo wanted to run away with Maria, but his father didn't give him any money, and it would have been difficult to put together the nine lire and fifty for a trip for two to Naples; they thought for a moment of suicide, but found that it would not solve their difficulties. Then, with the passing of time, their love became customary, the curses were always the same, and they couldn't go to bed without pouring on the faithful paper all the flood of their pain. In the small town, everybody was talking about their unshakeable love and their torments; they were the objects of general interest. If some tourist from Naples came, the townspeople led him to see the ruins of the amphitheater and told him the story of Carlo and Maria.

So the two young people, encouraged in their role of victims, assumed the proper attitude: Maria was always pale, with a melancholy air; never smiling; always talking to her friends of her days without joy; refusing to have fun; happy to look like a heroine of Mastriani. Carlo would go on solitary walks, always in a bad mood; at dances, he never moved from his corner, happy that around him people would whisper: "Poor young man, that unlucky love makes his life miserable!" In clubs, at parties, in visits, the tireless monotony of the small town would repeat endlessly the story of the two lovers, and those who had some fresh news on them were welcomed with open arms: Carlo and Maria were bearing with dignity the weight of their popularity.

Finally, I don't know after how many years—I believe four or five—of this constant struggle, of those daily tears, of this long-stretched love, kept alive by dissensions, things changed. There was a good person—there are still some of them—who, with many oratorical efforts, persuaded the parents that their lawsuits were costing them a lot of money (proof enough were the two lawyers who had become rich at the expense of their customers); that those two young people were miserable and would certainly fall ill because of that opposed love; their houses were next door to each other; next door their fields; Christ had forgiven, they should forgive, too, if they wanted to find forgiveness. He talked so much, and so many other people followed his example and intervened, that those quarrels reached an agreement, whose first order was the marriage of Carlo and Maria.

At this point, everyone will suppose that the two youths were very happy, and they would suppose correctly: But my duty as truthful storyteller forces me to say that their first allowed conversation found them greatly uneasy. They had become accustomed to seeing each other from far away, in a rush; to speak from the window on the ground floor to the street, in the dark, in a whisper. So they found each other very different, perhaps a bit ridiculous; they didn't have anything to say, so they often fell silent, looking forward to the moment when they would have to leave. There were no more imprecations and tears to be mixed with the ink; they didn't write to each other anymore. Everything was free, easy for their love: They didn't have to think about tricks to fool the surveillance of the old people, they no longer found pleasure in mumbling a few words in secret, they no longer made courageous projects for the future. They would marry dully, without obstacles, like so many other silly couples. The people in their small town no longer paid attention to them: Once the wonder and the comments on the marriage subsided, Carlo and Maria no longer attracted attention, nobody talked of them, nobody noticed their behavior. They ceased to be celebrated as an example of fidelity. Now everyone was looking at the wife of the Magistrate, who was accused of having a guilty sympathy for the Deputy Prosecutor of the King, a very serious crime. The two lovers felt abandoned, and a great coldness was born. Carlo found that the virtues of his fiancée, those virtues that were shimmering in her letters, became dull in the house. Maria often thought that Carlo was a bit vulgar in his tastes and that for such a stormy love to end up with a stupid marriage was unworthy of a reader of Mastriani. They had some lively exchanges over illusions disproved by reality, over miracles, optical deception, and other similar teasing; there was a quarrel, then two, then they became daily.

One evening Maria said in an irritated voice, "Carlo, let's end this."

"Yes, let's end it," he replied without hesitation.

The following day he left for an educational trip; Maria went to Naples, to visit her cousin, and to find herself a heroic husband. The families fell out again: Maria's father put a window in the wall facing the courtyard of his neighbor; in spite, the neighbor built a pigeon coop, whose pigeons fluttered everywhere; immediately there was a lawsuit, then a second, a third; the proceedings resumed, and this time, the lawyers said smiling, there was no hope for an agreement.

A LITTLE PLAY

In the park, in the woods, in the meadows, they had been walking for a long time. They had trampled a lot of fragrant grass, and the lady's shoes were infused with its smell; she complained of a little stone between the silk stocking and the sole. An infinite number of nervous lizards, crickets, and ants had been disturbed; indeed, speaking of the ants, the gentleman, moved by their sight, wanted to dedicate a poem to them. The July sun could have disturbed them, but the lady's umbrella was wide, the trees were full of leaves, and a light breeze blew from the west. Also, they were profoundly cheerful, with an inexhaustible humor, biting all human melancholies with a smile that in the lady was gay and sincere, and in the gentleman somewhat skeptical. These two people, whom on my and my readers' part I will declare unbearable, were still young and if not beautiful, jovial; they were alone, in the countryside, in the most beautiful season, and were not in love. Not even uneasy. They laughed, enjoyed themselves immensely, and walked arm in arm. They had made fun of many things together, especially of the soppiness of romance. They had mocked the eternal blond virgins that eternally tear up the petals of daisies; Paolo and Virginia, regarding the big umbrella of the lady; the famous butterflies in love, chasing each other over the hedges; the legendary nightingale singing among the branches; Catullus, whom the lady had not read and the gentleman had; the *Faute de l'abbé Mauret*, which both had read; all the more or less melancholy elegies, all the more or less colorful descriptions that have been written from time immemorial about the woods, the meadows and the flowers. How had they laughed about the tenacious ivy and the murmuring stream! The lady had the white little teeth of a mean kitten, the gentleman blond thin mustache with harmonious and seductive curves. They spent a merry morning. Their hearts were calm, their nerves steady, their spirits agile, their words lively.

With all the boldness of her character and the independence of her life, the lady was honest, peacefully honest: She had a husband in Milan, whom she loved and to whom she wrote every couple of days. She adored the sea and came to the beach in Castellammare. The gentleman had a wife, in Potenza, in Basilicata. He was very cold under his cheerful skepticism, having in the depths of his heart a silent contempt of the woman. That's why they were not in love; in short, without many explanations, they didn't love each other because they just didn't love each other. One could hardly give a reason for love, and it's the same thing for indifference.

"What if we had lunch?" the lady asked suddenly.

"Signora Lucia, you had an idea!" he said, feigning surprise.

"Be prepared, because I have another one. See what happens when I apply myself? It's an avalanche of ideas. Signor Federigo, let's go have lunch here, just a hundred feet away, at Giovannino's, in the thickets of roses and myrtles."

"Will he give us roses and myrtles for lunch? I am tormented by this doubt."

"Who knows? They told me that they have great food. At this time nobody will be there. Only crazy people like us go around. We will be horribly compromised in front of the waiter and the innkeeper..."

"Signora Lucia, the ruling classes must follow the rules of morality..."

"Enough, enough, for heaven's sake. Are you coming or not?"

"From the first moment you talked about breakfast, a sweet throb..."

"Rose in my poor heart..."

"A sweet image..."

"Seen through the fog of my dreams..."

"Seemed to come true..."

And they laughed again and walked in the dust of the main road, and did they swallow some dust! The afternoon was suffocating. The *Giovannino's* tavern, all white, had half-open shutters; it was utterly quiet.

"Signora Lucia, I am afraid there won't be any lunch for us here."

They looked at each other with a disappointed face. They were flustered from the heat. At that moment, a waiter with military trousers and a civilian jacket came to the door, looking at them with the greatest wonder. As they went up the stairs, he followed them.

"Should I prepare the meal in a particular room?" he asked then, as if speaking to himself, in a whisper.

Federigo hesitated for a moment, but she promptly, with a genuine laugh, turned and said, "Sure."

Later, left alone in the great hall, they were a little embarrassed. But it was just an instant. Right after, as the people of spirit they were, they understood the amusement of their position.

"Yes, madam," exclaimed Federigo, in a dramatic tone, "let us upset the honest conscience of this man."

"Let us scandalize him, indeed. We love each other, we are two guilty and happy people, about to have a tragic lunch, eating the rib of disgrace and drinking the wine of betrayal..."

"Madam, we are sinking into an abyss..."

"A bottomless abyss..."

"We may be caught. Oh, Lucia, I will shield you with my chest, especially as I don't have any other shields..."

"Why don't I have a veil, a long, black veil? What do you think, Signor Federigo, should I tremble and go pale?"

"Try, for a moment; I will endeavor to be agitated."

The waiter came to announce that the table was set. Signora Lucia got up, with a hurried step; Federigo followed her, talking to her in a whisper, telling her silly things that seemed to be love words. The waiter kept himself, as he should, at a distance. She, having arrived in the little room, let herself fall on a chair and hid her face in her hands very naturally.

"My friend, what do you want for lunch?"

"My friend, I'm not hungry," was her melancholy response.

"Will you drink Chablis?"

"Yes, yes," she said, with the hoarse voice and the wandering gaze of a woman madly in love.

The waiter left with their orders. They burst into laughing; they couldn't restrain themselves anymore. Lucia had tears in her eyes; Federigo hid his head in his napkin. What a funny thing! They were having fun like schoolboys on holiday. Then Lucia suddenly became serious. She looked around, a little disappointed. She couldn't find anything strange, anything new. He understood.

"Here we are in a small living room that has nothing special. Only in the novels you find the special ones. We are becoming bourgeois."

She smiled absently. He returned to play his part in their little comedy.

"What shall we do now, Signor Federigo, what shall we do to deceive this man? Invent something!"

"We'll have to address each other informally."

"It's true, it's true; indeed, let's pretend to get confused and embarrassed switching formal and informal address."

"Sure. Then, let's look at each other for a long time and stutter a few incomprehensible words..."

"When he talks to us, we'll pretend to be distracted, I will stare at the water in my glass..."

"And I'll make little balls of bread..."

The little comedy went on, wonderfully concerted, wonderfully played. The audience, composed of the waiter and the innkeeper, in the distance, in a hallway, fell for it. But for five minutes the actors enjoyed their roasted ribs, giving them their full attention.

"Signora Lucia, we shouldn't eat."

"Why?"

"You see, our heart is oppressed by guilt..."

"You're right.... indeed... But perhaps we will be those people who eat in anger..."

"And drink in despair..."

"To drown their remorse..."

Thus they continued their lunch with the good appetite of young people who have a calm soul and balanced health. But they didn't forget to play their parts.

"When he comes, Signora Lucia, we'll pretend to drink from the same glass."

"I will say, 'Federigo, do you remember Viareggio?'"

"And I will be moved, I will sigh, I will show immense regret."

They really enjoyed their little comedy; as they say in the theater, they got into their respective characters. They thought of what could be done better, more subtly. They looked at each other, wondering. In the small room, the summer heat was becoming unbearable. From the open window, with the half-closed shutters, not a breath of air was entering, but many flies were. Signora Lucia fanned herself; she had had two glasses of Chablis and their comedy excited her. Federigo remained calmer. After all, in both of them was the conscience of the clear divide between reality and comedy. They were not confused, no. They were not entering into greater intimacy because of their play; their mutual confidence was not increasing a bit. They were good friends, happy, satisfied of their mocking the innkeeper and the waiter. A perfect little play, indeed a real success. The waiter spoke softly, full of respect, and he walked making noise while approaching them, he walked silently going away. They smiled behind his back. Lucia peeled a peach, and cutting a piece of it, gave it to Federigo with a charming gesture of love: an idea that she came up with suddenly. Federigo took the piece of peach, lightly kissed the fingers of her little hand: this, too, an improvised idea. The waiter saw and pretended not to see: He slipped away to get coffee. They shook hands, exchanging their congratulations: In truth, they admired each other. They had never had so much fun in their lives.

What they did, they found it natural. Natural was their indifference, their impersonality. Indeed, they didn't even feel their position at all risky, so much was the serenity of their souls. They carried on like two children satisfied with a new game, found by chance. Federigo knew, because he had lived; Lucia guessed, because she was a woman. Anything unusual interested her.

"Signor Federigo, don't you think we should smoke cigarettes?"

"Lighting them, we'll exchange a look. Then we'll exchange the cigarettes."

"And we'll look at the smoke with a sad expression."

When the waiter came to clear the table, they smoked. A noise of wheels came from the street. Lucia cried out and let herself almost fall into Federigo's arms, trembling.

"My God, you'll kill yourself with these emotions..." he murmured, supporting her, cheering her up.

"It's a cart, madam," the waiter dared to say.

"All right, you can go," Federigo said sternly.

Oh, such amicable laughters! They would never find them again. They felt alive, refreshed in that July afternoon. They remained there, talking about so many pretty things, as in the park, joking about the ways of the whole world. They smoked. Every now and then the waiter passed by the ajar door, without looking in. They still smiled and took up the subject again. They left after an hour of conversation. They went down the stairs arm in arm. Turning around, they saw the waiter, the janitor, the cook, and the innkeeper all peering after them.

And they went off feeling light, rested and tranquil, disappearing in the dust of the street.

Back at the hotel, Signora Lucia slept deeply for three hours. In the evening, she didn't see Federigo in the Hall. The next morning, she received a letter from her husband, who called her back to Milan to go to the lakes. This gave her a great consolation, as Castellammare was starting to become boring. She wrote to Federigo a note of farewell, thanking him, and she set off, hurrying back home. Federigo read the note as he was shaving, shrugged and went to the bathroom.

***

For three years they didn't see each other, didn't know anything about the other. But the first night they met again, in that first moment, in a box of the Pergola Theater, in Florence, without a word, without a touch of their hands, in front of many people, they exchanged that burning look that makes the blood boil and forever joins lives. And the passion that overwhelmed them was a terrible storm.

CARNIVAL

The small room was immersed in darkness. Every so often, a reddish glow coming from the window was reflected on the wall. In the streets, groups of masked people wandered, torches in hand, singing, dancing, and cackling. Around eleven o'clock in the evening, a key turned in the lock. Magda entered, in the shadows; without turning on the light, she walked in the room, groping. A deep sigh lifted her chest.

"What a silence..." she muttered under her breath.

Thus she remained for a while, motionless in the middle of the room, like a black statue in the shadows. She allowed herself to be swallowed by that dark and deserted room.

"And how cold it is!" she added, shuddering.

Then, as if to escape from that gloom, she quickly lit two or three candles, threw some pieces of wood into the fireplace. With her delicate hands, she lifted the bellows and lit the fire. Immediately the room lit up. It was all gay in the light fabric of its red-flowered wallpaper, in its elegant furniture, in the lace of its boudoir. Gay in color, but deserted. Magda looked around. She was cold, every time she returned to wait in that lonely room for him to come. She only felt warm when he arrived; in fact, as soon as she heard his steps up the stairs, her hands burned like in a fever, her blood rose in a blaze to her face. Now she was freezing. Shivers passed over her white face, making her dark hair go limp. He had been missing from that room for ten days. She waited for him every day.

"Not even tonight he will come," she thought, loosening her magnificent hair to comb it.

But looking at herself in the mirror, she cheered up. She found that she was beautiful, with her red and fleshy lips, her green eyes that became phosphorescent in the evening, the spotless whiteness of her forehead and neck.

"He will surely come," she thought, reassured.

She forgot her cares while pulling and straightening her rich wavy hair that resembled the mane of a lion, lavishing on herself the most detailed care that a beautiful, rich, and unemployed woman can invent. The passing of a torchlight scared her.

"How many people in the streets..." she thought. "But he will surely come."

Yet with the passing of the hours, her anxiety grew. Her hands got tired, they moved slowly, then fell limply in her lap: Her whole person was gripped by a sense of infinite weakness.

"Take courage, he will come," she repeated to herself.

So she went to the carved wooden wardrobe and took out a complete Folly costume, half of blue satin, half of pink satin, all in silver bells, with a pointed cap, adorned with little bells. It was a short, low-cut, almost sleeveless costume. She put on her stockings, one of blue silk, one of pink silk, and the little boots, different from each other: the scepter full of bells was also ready. This set of clothing made her feel ashamed. She, who was used to trains of brocade and lace, to the severity of the velvets, was horrified by that despicable short dress worthy of a dancer, a rope jumper. She would never wear it, ever. She remained standing by the sofa, gazing at the dress with a pained expression. She would never have dared to wear it, ever.

Midnight chimed. She only had an hour to get dressed and go, one hour. Slowly, having to constantly sit down when taken by sudden fainting, raising again by sudden impulses, without looking in the mirror, blushing in her bare shoulders, from the neck to the forehead, shivering as if she had a fever. When she saw that under her skirt one could see her feet and all the way up to her knees, she threw herself on the sofa, all curled up, no longer daring to move. When she finally forced herself to pin the cap on her head and discovered that the smallest movement made all the little bells ring, she felt all the anguish of her ridicule. She would never go.

"It doesn't matter, he will come," she thought again, with mute heroism.

She put on her fingers the jeweled rings that made her hand look like something brightly winged, and she donned her black hooded satin cape, which completely enveloped her. Before leaving, she hesitated, as if she were abandoning a loved one forever. Everything seemed to tell her softly: *Stay, stay.*

"No, I will go," she said aloud, almost to encourage herself, "for he will come."

Only in the street did she feel the cold on her bare shoulders under the black satin of the cape; she, always used to being nice and warm, hadn't worn her fur. But as her devouring fever rose to her brain, she no longer felt cold. A new fear was that of not finding a carriage. She walked awkwardly and wary, frozen by the bitter cold, parched by the feverish heat, bumping into columns, losing her way with her vision impeded by her mask. Already some passersby had stopped in the street, staring at this uncertain, fragrant and elegant wooded cape. One of them had called to her, offering her dinner. She was trembling—she, the Countess, used to the devotion of her servants, to the respect of her friends—alone, abandoned, dying of shame and fear. Finally a carriage passed, and she called, and she climbed in like a shipwrecked man who reaches the shore.

"Who cares? He will come."

It was her mantra, her litany, her last, solemn, grandiose hope. It was a prayer: In him, her whole life was summed up. She didn't see the street, didn't notice the passing of time. She found herself in front of the atrium without knowing how she had arrived there. Stepping down from the carriage, on its threshold, a caped figure rudely complimented her on the beauty of her foot. She moved forward quickly inside the theater, not finding the hallway that would lead her to her box, lost, biting her lips in nervousness.

"Be patient, he will come."

When she arrived at her box it was one o'clock, the time set for the appointment. She looked carefully into the audience, where a dark and shouting crowd stirred, dressed in lively costumes and light colored capes. They danced, jumped, arms in the air, legs here and there, like noisy and unruly puppets. A reddish fog rose to the ceiling of the theater; it was difficult to distinguish faces. She strained her eyes through the mask, a strong emotion clouding her vision.

"He will come, he will come."

After exploring the stalls, she explored the boxes, one by one. Nothing.

"He will come, he will come, he will come."

She watched a very long, endless *galop*, whose dance line looked like a snake, now squashing its tail, now leaping, now breaking up. The whole hall was swept by the folly of the noise. One could hear the falsetto voices of the masqueraders who didn't want to be recognized. A shrill screech, an unseemly screaming. She felt frightened by it. All this seemed to her like a hellish dance, an orgy of the damned. She could never go down there, in the pit.

"He will come, he will come here."

Someone entered the box; Magda didn't know him. He spoke to her as to a lonely masquerader, looking for adventures; she went pale with indignation, she, the proud, indomitable Countess. She didn't answer. He, disappointed, ended up leaving. It was half past two.

"Maybe he is in the hall, and forgot the number of my box. Maybe I should look for him? Thus he will come."

Torn between fear and love, she slowly descended into the hall, looking for him. People called to her from every side, seeing her alone, hearing the damned and ridiculous tinkling of her bells: someone grabbed her by the arm, another bumped her, another yelled a word toward her white mask, another one whispered one to her ear. She resisted, pulled away, didn't answer, moved forward, half mad, always searching, like a wounded beast, with a fierce and humble look at the same time.

"He will come, he will come."

She didn't find him. Perhaps she didn't know how to look for him. Then she was assailed by the doubt that he had gone to her box while she was absent. She went up again, again waiting, dying a little every minute, shuddering at every trampling in the hallway, trembling in hearing any voice, stretching her gloves under her wide sleeves, unraveling the lace of her wooded cape.

"He will come."

****

At four o'clock in the morning, while the entire hall was swept by the last unbridled dance that had by now become a frenzy, Magda, in her Folly costume, short and revealing, cried silently under her mask, because he hadn't come, because he would never come.

DUALISM

I.

Flavia had a clean conscience: not even the shadow of a small remorse; what happened to her was very strange, but without a tiny bit of fault of her own.

So she would shake her beautiful blond head, she would shrug slightly, and go to the dance. Because then she fulfilled the obligations of her position with the best goodwill, indeed smiling at all times; at the parties, she danced from eleven o'clock in the evening till four o'clock in the morning, ripping carelessly her long trail, never tired. She never uttered those languid complaints about clothes that were too tight, heels that were too high, hats that were too big, like all other ladies; during the summer, she had a lot of fun on the beach, in improvised concerts, followed by the usual dances; in autumn, she liked the countryside, with hikes in the hills, fresh milk, chess games in the evening, the harvest of grapes and the hay; in winter, she would enjoy the theater and the long evenings. She would go without interval from a charity fair, to skating, throwing confetti, and sermons at the church of Gesù Nuovo. She was comfortable everywhere: A happy disposition if ever there was one; a young, blond, blue, serene youth. Two men loved her, she loved them both, but she didn't reproach herself. It was fatality, *ananke*, to say it in Greek.

The first—in temporal sense—was a young man, a sort of a relative, a sort of friend of Flavia's family; of equal condition in terms of wealth and nobility; he had the proud name of Leone, and almost to reflect his name—which in Italian means *lion*—he was a real aristocrat, from head to toe. He was not, however, the typical idle idiot, full of himself: Leone had heart and wisdom, not in exceptionally large quantities, but enough; and if he chose to put them at the service of the laws of his society, we should not blame him for that; he was born in that social class, and he didn't know how to break away from it. He was always courteous, always good and affable, with a pretty smile on his lips; some found him to be too predictable. Yet the respect he showed toward older women, the fact that he had never compromised a young one, a certain sense of loyalty that transpired from every action of his, would make people forgive him any even bigger fault. Above all, he shunned impulses, sudden enthusiasms, and passions without rule. A deep lover of peace, I don't think he aspired to great ambitions, to inaccessible heights; sublimity caused wonder in him, without attracting him. He had made a plan for a quiet, calm, easy life: He would first enjoy his free youth, and then he would marry, without too much hurry, a nice person. Meanwhile, he was looking for a nice person.

So one night, between a polka and a trip to the buffet, he made to Flavia a sort of declaration that came out of a compliment, whispered more than said. At the moment they laughed, they forgot about it; they saw each other again, they resumed their acquaintance, they got carried away: a stolen word, a hidden allusion, a special smile, a conversation stopped and resumed now and then, that's all. Yet that was love, love as they meant it: that is, gentle love, slightly scented, subtle, abandoned, resumed with a shadow of jealousy to reinforce it, but nothing more than a shadow; pale love, but a love which kept on living well, like many pale people.

It was enough for Leone's happiness that Flavia sent him every morning a pink note, with three lines in a delicate handwriting, the program of the day; it was enough for him that at the time of a chance encounter, she greeted him, with that bow of the head accorded to him alone; it was enough that at the dance she always reserved for him the first waltz; that before making a serious decision, such as the layout of a room, the colors of a dress, a trip in the countryside, he was consulted in that regard. For the rest, he left her free, he did not demand anything: He was always driven by the fear of ridicule, he kept in high regard appearances and didn't want to be seen as the ugly figure of the jealous lover; he never resented the many admirers surrounding Flavia. In fact, I would say that he felt sort of happy; he knew that the world knew, and that was enough to reassure him.

The girl, too, was easily satisfied: to find him punctual at their meetings, always the first one to arrive, to listen to those sweet words he could say so well, to see in his buttonhole a flower like the one she put in her hair, and to impose on him, occasionally, some little whim, to see him obey with a graceful smile, to receive that half-hidden, exquisite, delightful courtship, which didn't impose any obligation on her. The people around murmured: *A beautiful couple!* Her relatives were not displeased.

In the case of Flavia, fatality was called Everardo, and he lived on the fifth floor of her building. The clever reader will understand that he is a poet, and it is the truth, but I must add, to lessen the bad impression, that his verses were good, though they were not read by anyone. He belonged to a class that is numerous in all major cities, because every year a large number of good and willing young people arrive in all major cities. They have their heads full of wonderful fantasies and beautiful plans, their heart overflowing of affections and their purse not overflowing at all. To the poor and good dad who remained behind in the little village, they promised to attend Cujacio, to be introduced to Euclid, to build a close relationship with Tiesot and Orfila. Promises. But these poetical lurkings come from the lessons of literature, from the youth associations, the literary circles, the lively discussions about art; all this feeds the bravery of someone who is twenty years old. And so... so a whole category of displaced people is formed, and out of it comes the young boy, pale, skeptical, impatient to reach a goal for which almost always he will not have enough strength, torn by the desire to arrive, devoured by ambition, unable to return to the old and straight road, tortured by an unequal struggle that makes him deeply unhappy. And his dad is always in his village, working, sacrificing, hoping that his child will be happy, will build a position for himself... and you don't know which of the two is more worthy of compassion—the sweet illusion of the old man, or the desolate disillusion of the young man. Thus geniuses are born, they say, I know; but for one genius born, thousands of mediocre men agonize.

It would be better if the genius were born otherwise.

This is the story of Everardo. Add to that a passionate heart, an irritable nervous system, a pair of burning eyes, and you will have a portrait of him. Naturally, he met Flavia on the marble staircase, on a dark autumn day with a diffused and sad light, but Flavia was blond and smiled. Noticing that she was coming down the stairs, the poor poet had the impression that this girl was descending from above, was a ray of rosy light, playful, lost in that dusk. He said nothing, didn't move. She passed, but took away with her the soul of a man.

I am not going to recount how seeing Flavia again only made Everardo fall deeper and deeper in love with her; how he described in a fiery letter all this love and the many difficulties he had to overcome before the letter finally reached her little hands. Suffice to say, he was successful in his intent. Flavia read those brief words twice and remained thoughtful, with furrowed eyebrows and a serious expression. The letter burned her fingers as lit coal, yet she did not put it down. She had the impression that those words were flames, caressing her hand, and penetrating in her veins; she felt a great heat invading all of her, reaching her heart and her brain, flowing in her blood; she thought she was surrounded by the splendid and dazzling light of the afternoon. No feeling of pain—in fact, she enjoyed that rich and sweet fire in which her soul melted. She thought of Leone, and she thought of Everardo: She loved them.

II.

There were times when Flavia felt invaded, surrounded by a great gentleness, as if voices high and far sang for her a sweet song, as if the hands of children were showering her head with flowers. She felt vague instincts, floating, undecided aspirations: She wished for soft, temperate colors, where the pale shades evaporate like a caress; small rooms where the temperature is lukewarm like a human breath, where noises goes out in the soft wool of carpets; warm and scented textures, slightly rustling, surrounding the body, as if loving it and breathing with it; the subtle smells that rock the nerves in a delightful half-sleep. And on the pink-blue background of these dreams a slight shadow appeared, which then became more distinctive—it was Leone. A beautiful, noble, rich, gentleman in love, bloodline of princes: With him, life was to be a long and inexhaustible celebration, a series of happy, smiling days, without ever the bitterness of tomorrow, without a sorrow, without a black spot. Flavia loved him; when from her carriage she saw him ride on his English horse with its proud head and steel hocks, her heart lifted toward the handsome and elegant knight; when she saw his proud glance become loving while staring at her, when he spoke in a whisper, she felt an irresistible fascination. Leone was for her a whole world, a high world, even above misfortune, where one enjoys the satisfaction of the most refined tastes, the deep and secure calm of wealth, the infinite and varied flattering of luxury. Leone was peace—a tranquil joy, a quiet life.

29

And in the certainty of Leone's love she cradled her heart, falling asleep.

The awakening was sudden, quick: All of her being would jump, shaken by an internal force; she got up, walked, wanted to break something in her hands, felt her head too small. She had tumultuous and contrasting thoughts, broad and bold ideas, a clear need for action and combat. At that time, she understood how sublime is the silent work of the poet and thinker; she understood how art could be the only supreme desire of a man, she comprehended the unbridled wish for glory; to be low, to be poor, unknown, lost in the crowd, an unknown atom in a huge mass, and all the while to look up, to soar, glitter, to be the one: Everardo. With him, a lively, omnipotent passion, a love that is unique, that dominates everything, that overcomes any obstacle, soothes every defeat, enlarges every victory. The obscure poet worshiped the noble maiden who descended from her heights to delight him with her affection, and she was conscious, proud of this blind love, which was infused by the most proud jealousy. When Flavia was at the dance, she knew that there was a man in the dark and lonely street that was filled with impatience, who envied even the lowest servant in that house flooded with light. And in the golden halls, among the waving of the fabrics and the smiles of women, she, seized by a crazy idea, wished to leave everything, flee down the stairs, throw herself to his neck and say, "I love you; take me away."

When she thought of Everardo's difficult and poor life, of the small and low room where in winter he suffered bitter cold, of the continuing privations he was subjected to, of all those scary details of a terrible misery, she felt for him a great admiration, for in that environment he remained a poet, full of faith, always caressing hopes, still dreaming of his ideal. Flavia felt very humiliated in the face of that courage, she who could not give up the extravagant and empty luxury, the unnecessary jewels, the expensive fashion. How did she hate all these things, how did she hate them! She would have liked to renounce them, to punish her body used to living in those luxuries, to expose herself to cold, hunger, and bring also into her heart that treasure of strength and youth. To marry the poet, to be the life of his life, to pass through all his anxieties, to share his life full of thrills, battles, and sorrows!

Thus, in the careless and cheerful girl played the wonderful drama of dualism. There were two equally strong and opposing powers; her inclinations, up until then indistinct and confused, detached themselves, taking the opposite course. She lived passing through these consecutive states of mind, one the opposite of the other, which would in turn be destroyed, to re-emerge more vigorous and start fighting again. Yet she did not suffer for it; indeed, in this strange phenomenon of her spirit, she felt complete and satisfied, almost as if she had regained her psychological balance. That constant sway left her calm; it was her natural state, and it was explainable.

Flavia was born of a mixed marriage: Her father was very high in society, her mother very low, and each of them had given her their own nature. She had in her the robust temper of her mother, her simple and great tastes, her desire to fight, her honest and lively throb, her wholesome and lively people's spirit. From her father, she had superficial feelings: the weakness of the nerves, the gentle aspirations. In short, two consciences; but these two consciences had merged, creating one, and in the same way her two loves were reduced to one, and Flavia was happy, very happy, having found in the most absurd way the unity of her spirit.

III.

The two who had met and merged so well in the heart of the girl, meeting in real life and knowing to be rivals, looked at each other angrily: Leone took Everardo for a courageous madman, Everardo took Leone for a proud fool. Certainly they could not understand and much less appreciate each other: They agreed in only one, spontaneous gesture, because on the following day Flavia received two almost identical letters whose message could be summarized with one word: *Choose*.

The girl was painfully surprised, felt a deep affliction in her heart, as if she had been announced a great misfortune. She thought she was having one of those terrible dreams in which you fall, always fall from a great height, and the anguish extends to your awakening. *Choose*. She had to choose. Why? She had felt so much enjoyment, and her life had been so complete and full in that love! *Choose*. Whom? She felt she loved them equally, she felt that both of them were necessary to her, she couldn't even imagine having to erase one of those names from her mind, to erase one of those images from her soul. It was impossible, impossible, impossible. She was asked for something unjust, she was angry for demand. Everything fell, everything fell, everything plunged into nothingness. That beautiful harmony was disturbed and broken, peace had disappeared, and she had to choose: to love one alone, to sacrifice one's affection to the other, to suffocate one of her consciences, to die by half. She wanted to do so, wanted to decide. She accumulated the arguments that she had to defend and to make prevail one of the two young men over the other. She even made a decision and tried to strengthen herself to carry it on, but it was useless: The next moment she thought of the other man. She spent miserable days, tired, hopeless, assailed by cruel doubts, abandoned to tormenting hesitations. She fell in an unbearable state. So she preferred the complete abandonment, the total break: She rejected all love, renounced both of them. Leone and Everardo judged her a common flirt, but she did not care to explain to them the mystery of her heart.

The blond girl suffered much, spent sleepless nights and the melancholy days, but even pain tends to diminish and disappear. For her, love had become a far-away remembrance, a happy and past era, a beautiful and exhausted period; sometimes she thinks of it, but with no wish to relive it. Like many people on this earth, she loved what is enough: In her two loves, she summed up her great love.

MIDDLE CLASS COMEDIES

When they met on the street, the two girls kissed each other with great noise, and they looked each other up and down to observe the respective hairstyles and give very discreet but not very charitable comments; at the church of the Madonna delle Grazie, where they listened to the Mass with their respective families, they exchanged an amiable smile from afar, while one mentally calculated the price of the new hat of the other, and the other consoled herself with the spite of the one; in the morning, they said hello from their balconies, which faced over Via Speranzella: Pasqualina maliciously noticing that Mariuccia had gotten up half an hour later than usual, as the true lazy bum she was, and Mariuccia telling herself that Pasqualina had bags under her eyes and a pale face when she got out of bed, a sign of youthful freshness fading. At the balls, they always remained close: in appearance because they loved each other, but in reality to keep a close eye on each other. If Pasqualina began a crochet work, Mariuccia immediately started the embroidery of a tapestry; if Mariuccia learned to torment the *Bellissima* tune by Coop on the piano, Pasqualina soon started to torture the *Povera* by the same master. Pasqualina possessed a gold medallion with the word *Souvenir* in black enamel, but Mariuccia wore on her little finger a ring with two beads and a turquoise; Mariuccia had a gray silk dress, garnished in blue, and Pasqualina had a green one, garnished in black. Pasqualina was blond and pretended to love brown hair, while she actually despised it; Mariuccia was a brunette and praised blonde hair, while she could not bear it.

In short, they ran after each other, the tormented each other, spied on each other, met, remained for a moment in balance, would break off again, and begin again the race, with a concentrated and hidden ardor. So, at first sight, seeing the interest that one had for the other, it seemed that they loved each other tenderly, and people believed it, but in essence, they were rivals, fierce rivals, of that stifled, crude, energetic, and cruel rivalry, of that ferocious rivalry which is one of the many dramas stirring in the apparent placidity of middle-class life.

The lucky cause of this feud was Arturo Pietraroia, a young man of twenty, very far from being the hero of a novel, but who had become such for the two girls. First of all, his name was Arturo, which is of great poetic value among people who responded to the respectable, yes, but prosaic names of Bartolomeo, Bernardo, Gaetano, Rocco, Donato, and so on. Then, his status of being the legitimate son of Roberto Pietraroia, a shopkeeper in knick-knacks, with a large four-door bazaar in Via Roma, gave him a deeply heroic and interesting character. The young man showed a slight contempt for oil merchants like Pasqualina's father, for those leather merchants like Mariuccia's father, for those of salted cod, flour, sugar—coarse people who deal with ignoble things. His father's business was something fine, distinct, and he carried in his whole person the reflection of this finery, of this distinction. The slanting pose of his head resembled those of the white porcelain figurines that were sold in the warehouse; he bowed like some Pompadour marquises, painted on the satin of the fans priced at eight lire and fifty each; he smiled ironically, like a Florentine bronze Mephistopheles for candelabrum, to whom a meager and lanky Don Quixote was a companion; he had a vapid attitude, a light gait, the light and careful hand of someone used to touch fragile objects always. Always a very open collar, which is the mark of the shop assistant; absurdly colorful ties, mostly of a deep red, and on the tie every two days a new pin, of fake gold, but patented for perfect gold imitation, pins with the strangest and most ridiculous shapes: a fork, a lizard, a nutcracker with the walnut represented by a fake pearl, a triangle with the Masonic symbol, a large nail. The chain of the watch was now made of hammered steel, now of burnt silver, now of braided Russian leather, now of twisted black silk cord, now it was the real chain of security against thieves; funnel-shaped cuffs rained over the fingers, closed by huge buttons, which followed the same variability of the pin and the chain. In his pockets, a cigar case of painted straw, a black leather wallet with a group of violets embroidered in silk, a mother-of-pearl purse with his initials, a match holder of faux platinum. In the summer, a cane of gutta-percha, in winter an umbrella from a knick-knack shop, in bad silk, with fabulous handle and knob; in his handkerchief a strong and coarse scent, which one could smell a mile away. In short, in his person was all the dubious elegance of the bazaar, the noisy and clamorous luxury—all things that dazzled and fascinated the two bourgeois maidens.

As for the rest, the boy also enjoyed other seductions. He spoke with nonchalant pride of the rich carriages that stopped in front of his shop, of the beautiful ladies who came from them, the duchess such-and-such who had come to buy a tea service for twenty-four people and had relied solely on his taste, yes, on *his* taste, Arturo Pietraroia's; the little countess so-and-so who had come to buy an album for portraits and whose fingertips he had squeezed in handing it to her; and she had accepted his gesture, even smiled— and all the ladies, entering the store would walk straight to him, they wanted to be served by him, preferring him the other three clerks—and he bowed, spoke French, led the ladies back to the carriage door.

All of which made Pasqualina and Mariuccia quiver with pleasure and at the same time made them angry with jealousy. Arturo posed as a Don Giovanni, knew by name all the more or less ugly florists in Naples, bumped all seamstresses in the street, offering them gallant words and allowing a glimpse of a thousand amorous and mysterious adventures under a transparent veil of modesty, which put the two girls in a constant anxiety, afraid of seeing him kidnapped at any moment. Arturo, on Sunday dressed up, curled his hair, put a flower in his buttonhole, donned a pair of dragon-blood colored gloves, and drove in his carriage to the Riviera di Chiaia. Arturo was the best director of those eminently stupid games, which with an expressive phrase are called *games of penitence*, and made his spirit shine in them, a shopkeeper and insolent spirit that sent the people around him into a craze; he was a very capable dancer of those family quadrilles that employ a maximum of eight couples, and he sported an openly Neapolitan French pronunciation, but whose guttural *r* gently tickled the ears of the dancing ladies. For these merits and many more, which I will omit for the sake of brevity, Arturo Pietraroia turned over and over the keys of the hearts of Pasqualina Rubinacci and Mariuccia Jandoli.

But if the two girls were in love with him, with whom was this gentleman in love? With both? With neither one? Silence! Mystery!—as in the opera librettos. Arturo's behavior with the two young girls was so cleverly balanced, so impartial in the distribution of his graces, that if we wanted to try to see clearly in it, we would lose our minds, and they lost their heads. For example: One Sunday, at Mass, he went to the nave where Pasqualina was, and gave her long, languid looks. Pasqualina triumphed and Mariuccia gnawed with rage. But in the evening, at the Villa, by the stand where the band plays, he sat in the Jandoli family group, near Mariuccia, courting her in a clear and open way. For the whole week, he would go for a walk with the brother of Pasqualina, speaking to him informally, treating him confidently, giving him cigars and coffee, as if they were future brothers-in-law. Then for fifteen days he would be always seen with Don Bernardo Jandoli, talking to him about leather, writing a complaint against income tax for him, asking him how the business went, with other similar gracious commercial expressions. One evening he would praise blond hair and looked at Pasqualina; another he glorified black eyes and stared at Mariuccia. It was a continuous game of swings, a succession and an alternation of equal and opposite phrases, a regular and constant contradiction. As soon as one of them believed she had conquered him, she lost him. A victory had barely the time to assert itself, and was immediately followed by a defeat. The certainty of the definitive conquest didn't last more than one day, sometimes no more than an hour. Afterward, it was immediately put in doubt by a new move of the fickle knick-knack shopkeeper. In this tormenting game, in these strokes of spurs, in these whiplashes, the rivalry of the two girls would become increasingly stronger, their souls would be provoked, they would be incited to fight, and the secret that they kept served to increase hatred more than love. After eight months, neither of them had progressed one step; Arturo had not compromised himself with a dangerous word, and the girls had arrived to the point of using extreme remedies.

Extreme remedies, indeed: They set in motion all the small resources of bourgeois coquetry, sought all the means to reach the heart of the trinkets seller, in order to arrive to a decision. Large quantities of purple rice powder were used, at fifty cents a packet; the old ribbons of the unused hats were made into hair ties, bows for the neck; Pasqualina worked a crochet lace, in yellow thread, and decorated a dress with it. Mariuccia embroidered strips of fine cotton for the same purpose. Both spent their nights in secret work, stimulated and driven by a fixed thought. Mariuccia borrowed some novels from Arturo: *The Blind of Sorrento* by Mastriani, *The Count of Montecristo*, hiding them from her parents, to be able to talk about them with him. Pasqualina sacrificed her blonde fringe on the forehead, and set her hair according to the fashion of the last six months and bought a turtle comb. On the day of the Assumption,

Mariuccia sent a sweet cake, made with her own hands, to Donna Assunta Pietraroia, mother of the hero, to let her admire her domestic and culinary virtues; Pasqualina maneuvered to let Roberto Pietraroia, father of the hero know, indirectly, that she was an expert in accounting. Alas! All was useless. The hero didn't make up his mind; he remained cold, perhaps delighting in the loving homage of the two girls. Perhaps he had a purpose.

Finally, no longer knowing what to do, Pasqualina poured her sorrows into the bosom of Donna Mariantonia Lomonaco, a widow for the third time, with a beautiful mustache, a great matchmaker, cursed by five or six unhappy couples, but who continued her civilizing mission with great zeal.

And Mariuccia, at her wits' end, confided in Carminella, an old servant of the house, an expert woman, of proven loyalty, who promised her to carry out this delicate and dangerous mission.

***

"Well, my dear Pasqualina," said Donna Mariantonia Lomonaco, in a solitary conversation that she had arranged, inviting the girl to dinner, "I gathered information and I assure you, my dear, that it took some doing. Finally I was able to find a sister-in-law— the cousin of Assunta Pietraroia—and I managed to discover everything. The party is not a good one. The store is doing badly, very badly, especially since in Via Roma, four more have opened. It still holds for the credit it has, earns the daily minimum, but it doesn't pay the bills on time. Don Roberto and Donna Assunta hope that the son will fall in love with some daughter of a solid shopkeeper, who will bring a dowry five or six thousand ducats, which would be invested in the shop and serve to raise their fortune. The party is a handsome young man; he knows of his parents' intentions and approves them. If you, my dear, want to put your dowry in knick-knacks, if you think it is a good use of money, you do it. If you are in love with the young man, it is another story. I have also known love—" added Donna Mariantonia Lomonaco, sighing like a bellows. "And I know what it is. Otherwise, there is another solid party, a young goldsmith, Vincenzino Scotti."

***

"My dear lady, my dear lady," Carminella began saying with emphasis and with a great deal of gestures, "to serve you I have turned over half the world. Finally, through my confessor, a holy priest who confesses also the porter woman of the Pietraroia house, I was able to make friends with her and now I can say that we are very close. She told me everything, from top to bottom: All sincere words, how true is the day of today, the day of the glorious St. Nicholas! It is not for you. Listen to me: Leave it alone. In the Pietraroia house, there is always war, they quarrel from morning to night. Donna Assunta reproaches her husband for the dowry that he has invested in the bazaar. Don Roberto returns home always in a bad mood, a sign that business is bad at the warehouse. Day by day, they show off with big spending, but the shopkeepers out of town seem to no longer want to send their stuff to sell. Don Roberto and Donna Assunta put their hopes only in that son—that

41

he could make some young lady with a dowry fall in love with him and so manage to go on. My dear lady, the Blessed Virgin, that immaculate Virgin, must enlighten you and make you forget that young man. He is not a good party for you: With this beautiful face, with the dowry you bring, you deserve better luck. Don Leonardo, the first clerk of your father, always had a weakness for you…"

***

Pasqualina clasped her hands in the muff, with a slight shiver of cold.

"Are you cold?" Mariuccia asked, bending towards her, attentive.

"Yes, a little. Dad said that this cold that will hurt the business."

"My dad said the same. The warehouses were hoping to do good business in these Christmas and New Year's holidays…"

"Also the Pietraroias were hoping for it," Pasqualina added indifferently.

"I heard they are doing very poorly," said Mariuccia in the same tone.

"Very. My dear, the business of trinkets is not a safe business. You risk, you risk…and then! You end up losing money."

"So it is."

A silence followed. Mariuccia took courage and

uttered the big sentence. "Also, that Arturo is a madcap."

"You are so right! A mindless dude."

"Running after every skirt."

"In that warehouse there are constantly ladies coming and going..."

"A poor girl, in addition to bringing him the dowry, which would have been in danger, should also fear..."

"Imagine, my dear! As for me, I pity the poor girl who will find herself there."

"I do, too."

"And... tell me, is there anything for you?" Mariuccia asked, smiling.

"Eh!... Who knows... maybe... nothing certain yet. And what about you?"

"Nothing certain... maybe there is something..."

"Hopefully soon."

"Let's hope. Something solid, yes?"

"Goldsmith and jeweler. And you?"

"Somebody in leather, like dad."

"Good luck, my dear. I've always loved you!"

"And I you! Like a sister! Good luck."

LULÙ'S TRIUMPH

I.

Sofia didn't raise her eyes from her work, and her light fingers flew over the delicate lace. Instead Lulù moved about the room, moved the objects on the shelves, opened a drawer to look in, distracted; it was clear that she wanted to do or say something, but her sister's serious countenance made her uncomfortable. She tried to hum a little song, she declaimed a poem; Sofia didn't seem to hear her.

So Lulù, who didn't have much patience, resolved to face the problem, and standing in front of her sister, asked her, "Sofia, do you know what Mademoiselle Jannette told me?"

"Nothing very interesting, for sure."

"Here we go again, with your dry and cold responses that cause chills in summer! Where do you get your coldness, my frosty sister?"

"Lulù, you really are a child."

"Here where you are wrong, my beloved, older sister; I'm not a little girl, because I'm getting married.

"What?"

"That's what Jannette told me."

"What fraud! I don't understand it at all."

"Right now, I'll tell you everything, as they say in the plays. It will be quite a story…but is Your Seriousness going to give me all her attention?"

"Yes, yes, but hurry up."

"The moment and the place of this story: the day at the horse races in Campo di Marte. You were not there, since you prefer your blessed books…"

"If you keep digressing, I won't listen to you anymore."

"You have to listen to me; this secret stifles me, kills me…"

"Are you doing it again?"

"I'm stopping, I'm stopping. I was saying, at the races we were in the front row on the grandstand. Paolo Covato arrives and introduces us a handsome young man, Roberto Montefranco. Usual greetings and nice compliments, they find their seats and sit behind us, exchange a few words until the signal for the departure of the horses is heard. You'll remember that I was favoring Gorgona, without foreseeing how much that horse would have been ungrateful…we must also resign ourselves to the ingratitude of the beasts. A cloud of dust makes the horses disappear. 'Gorgona wins,' I exclaim.

"'No,' Montefranco says, smiling, 'Lord Lucello wins.' I get annoyed by that contradiction, he continues to smile and contradict me; we make a bet. Finally, after half an hour of racing heartbeat and anxiety, I come to know that Gorgona is a traitor, that I lost and Montefranco won: Imagine! I tell him that I want to pay my debt right away. He bows and says that there is time; I meet him at Chiaja, I give him a questioning look; he just greets me, and smiles in a mysterious way. So at the theater, so everywhere: I live in the utmost curiosity: Roberto is beautiful, he is twenty-six years old…and this morning Mr. Montefranco Senior, my future father-in-law, was in conference for two hours with our mother."

"Oh!"

"My public gives signs of paying attention. I heard from Janette the news of his father. So the marriage is agreed upon. It remains to be decided a very important thing: When I will go to the vice-mayor, will I have a gray or dead-leaf colored dress? Will I wear my hat with or without scarves?

"You are too hasty…"

"Hasty? Of course: There are no obstacles. Roberto and I are madly in love, our dear parents are happy…"

"And you marry would marry a man in such a way?"

"What do you mean by *such a way*? That is quite an ambiguous expression…"

"I mean without knowing him, without loving him?"

"But I do know him, I saw him at the horse races, and while walking! I adore him! The day before yesterday, just because I hadn't seen him, I refused to have breakfast and I drank three cups of coffee to try to commit suicide."

"And what about him?"

"He is marrying me, so he must love me!" Lulù replied victoriously.

But seeing Sofia's face go pale, Lulù regretted that imprudent phrase and, bending over her sister, asked her with affection: "Did I say something mean?"

"No dear, no, you're right, who loves gets married. The difficult thing is to make ourselves be loved," and she sighed lightly.

"'To make ourselves be loved!'" Lulù repeated, annoyed. "It's quite easy, Sofia; but when, like you, one has a frown on the face, sad eyes and unsmiling lips, when stays in a corner to think, while everyone else dances and jokes, when instead of laughing one reads, and instead of living one's dreams, when one is young but looks tired and old, then it is difficult for one to be loved."

Sofia lowered her head and didn't answer. Her lips trembled and she stifled a sob.

"Have I hurt you again?" Lulù asked. "The fact is, I want to see you loved, surrounded by affection, and marred ... What a pleasure if we married on the same day!"

"Foolishness! I will remain a spinster."

"Not for the world, I forbid it, bad girl. If Roberto is a gentleman, he must have a celibate brother; I want him!"

At that moment their mother came in, dressed to go out.

"Are you going out, Mom?" Said Lulù.

"Yes, dear, I am going to see our lawyer."

"Uh! The lawyer! Serious stuff this is!"

"You'll find out, you joker. Sofia, come with me for a moment."

"Is Sofia also having dark dealings with the lawyer?"

"When will you learn to be serious?"

"Soon, Mom, you'll see." She opened the door at the passage of her mother and sister, and made two deep curtsies, murmuring, "Madam, Miss…"

When they passed through the door, she cried out, laughing, "Speak, speak, you two! I'll pretend I know nothing!"

II.

Roberto Montefranco usually didn't think much: He didn't have time. His days flew by him, with breakfast, horse riding, visits, lunch. His evenings were spent sweetly at Lulù's, his fiancée.

Then there were the little things to do, a few meetings with the lawyer, some contracts to sign, some old debts to pay; add to that the preparations of the home and the honeymoon. He barely had half an hour to read and a quarter of an hour to waste in a café. So he was never seen absorbed in profound reflections, nor he was known to have ever been busy solving some social problem, for Roberto had nothing tragic or heroic in his temperament.

Indeed, he enjoyed a serenity of spirit envied by many.

One day, in the afternoon, he lay on the armchair, one leg crossed over the other, a toothpick in the mouth, and a book in hand, with the precise determination of reading. The book was interesting; but because of a new and unexpected case—the reader was very distracted; I will say more: He was nervous and restless. He never turned the page because after a couple of lines, the letters came out of place, jumped, got confused, disappeared. Roberto, unwillingly, was leaving for the unknown regions of thought.

Dad is satisfied, my aunts send me their holy blessing, my cousins are angry, my friends at the café congratulate me ironically, my serious friends shake my hand—so I am doing the right thing getting married? One couldn't deny that Lulù is very pretty; when she looks at me with those eyes full of malice, when she laughs showing her white teeth, I want to grab that fair head of hers and give her many, many kisses! She also has a beautiful, a gold disposition, always happy, always in a good mood, ready for a joke, full of spirit, never picky, never melancholy. We will get along; I can't stand pensive faces, especially in the people I love; it seems to me that they always hide a secret suffering, a suffering that I don't know and I can't soothe, or perhaps of which I am the involuntary cause. Sofia, my future sister-in-law, has the gift of irritating me with her cold and impassive face: When she appears, my soul closes, the smile dies on my lips, and even if the most beautiful spring sun was shining, it would seem to me to be in a dark and gray November day. I don't even have the courage to joke with Lulù any more; that Sofia dispels any joy. She probably became aware of the bad effect she has on me, because she greets me without looking at me, doesn't offer me her hand, she answers with short phrases, became aware of my dislike. Maybe she is sorry about it.

Lulù always laughs. She is very young. She never speaks a word in seriousness, and even if she tries to, she doesn't succeed and seems to want to joke. She says she loves me, and then she laughs and talks about something else. She loves me, but it's not a desperate love. In conscience, not even my love for her is so desperate.... better this way. For what I am concerned, I have two clear theories, set in my mind: First, the two to be married need to have the same disposition; second, you should never start with a strong passion. This is just the case with Lulù; we will be extremely happy. We'll go on a trip around Italy, but without running, without rushing, in short legs, enjoying all the comforts, stopping where we like, admiring even the smallest things. It will take at least three months...no, it's not enough...let's say four. I'd like take Lulù away, for a time, from the sad company of Sofia. But, I wonder, is it natural that a girl should be so serious at this age? She is probably twenty-three…she's not ugly, I guess. Indeed, she has beautiful eyes and a queen-like demeanor. If she wasn't so severe, she could be liked. I foresee she will remain a spinster; maybe this is her trouble, maybe a love... a betrayal... I would be so curious to know the cause of her sadness... I'll ask her when we find ourselves alone...

.... Lulù likes sweets, she told me so the second night that I went to her house. One has to see how she gnaws on them; they liquefy, they disappear behind those red lips, and after a while she assume an air of false regret, when she says that there are no more. She's so pretty! She confided to me, in a whisper, that when it thunders she is afraid, and goes hiding her head under the pillows; that she has always dreamed of having a black velvet dress, long, with a white lace on its sleeves and neck; she assured me that she will be jealous, jealous of me like a Spanish girl, and she will buy a small dagger with a steel handle and gold inlay to exact her revenge. She is adorable when she says these things in her childish and assertive tone. Even Sofia is forced to smile, sometimes—the smile lights up her face... That Sofia! That Sofia! Who will ever come to know her soul? ...

The book fell from his knees to the ground, our young man was startled by its noise, looked stunned, almost didn't recognize himself. It was really he, Roberto Montefranco, caught in a flagrant meditation crime.

III.

Dusk fell like a fine drizzle of gray ash; Sofia,

standing behind the balcony windows, looked down into the crowded and noisy road. It was the time when Via Toledo becomes dangerous for the large numbers of small and large carriages crossing it, constantly, without rest. Sofia seemed to look for someone. Suddenly, a vivid blush appeared on her face, she bowed her head a little, became pale, and immediately went back to her bedroom. Less than a minute later, Lulù came in like a storm, slamming doors, shifting chairs to run better.

"What are you doing here, Sofia Santangelo? Were you reading?"

"Yes... I was reading."

"Didn't you stay on the balcony?"

"And what if I did?"

"Well! I had to stay in my room because Albina, the seamstress, has brought me the dress for tonight. Meanwhile, I was impatient because I wanted to be here. Last night I told Roberto to put on his blue coat, attach Selin at the carriage, and pass by at six thirty. I wonder if he obeyed me…"

"Roberto passed with his blue coat, on his carriage."

"Mercy! How do you know all this? Weren't you reading?"

"I was behind the window."

"And you recognized Roberto, though you never look at him? Miracle! Did he greet you?"

"Yes."

"Did he take his hat off?"

"Why... he always does."

"And did you answer?"

"Do you take me for a rude person?"

"Did you smile at least?"

"No... I mean, I don't know."

"You're a bad girl, Sofia. Even last night Roberto was talking about you..."

"Did he tell you I was a bad girl?"

"No, he was just asking me the reason of your introverted disposition, so different from mine. So in your defense I started praising you; I told him that you are better, more lovable, and more loving than I, and that you have the defect only of hiding your qualities. Imagine, he listened to me with great interest. Finally, he asked me about your aversion to him..."

"Aversion!"

"So he said, and you know, he's not so wrong! You treat him with so little friendliness! But even on this point I defended you, I told him a lie, that is that you like him, and esteem him so much..."

"Lulù!"

"I know it's not true; but Roberto loves you so well,

is it not ungrateful to treat him like a stranger?"

Sofia threw her arms around her sister's shoulders and kissed her; Lulù held her close for a moment, and murmured in a caressing voice, "Why don't you love Roberto, at least a little?"

The other made an abrupt movement, pulling back, and didn't say a word.

"So," Lulù said, shrugging and changing topic, "are you sure you don't want to come with us tonight?"

"No, I have a headache, you can go with Mom."

"As usual. All right, I'll go all the same, because I'll have a lot of fun."

"Is he coming with you... Roberto?"

"No, he's going to his club, where there is a meeting of the Board of Directors. I take advantage of it to escape and dance until morning."

"And does he know that?"

"Even better if he does, he'll learn to leave me my freedom. I don't want him to take on bad habits."

"You don't love him very much, it seems to me."

"I do, very much, but in my own way. But I need to go and dress; it will take me at least two hours."

***

Sofia listened to the noise of the carriage moving

away, carrying her mother and sister; she was alone, as she always wished to be. As a child, when someone wronged her, she would weep only when she was in bed, in the dark, and that habit had never left her. Now, lost in that great salon, under the clear light of the lamp, her hands still and her head resting on the back of the chair, she showed on her face a great affliction, a lively reflection of her great internal struggle. Certainly in those moments of complete solitude, a great sorrow would surface to her consciousness; the sense of the long-rejected reality would become clear, distinct, cruel.

The sound of steps startled her. It was Roberto. Seeing her alone, he stopped, hesitant; but assuming the rest of the family in another room, he advanced. Sofia immediately stood up, troubled.

"Good evening Miss."

"Good evening..."

They were both uneasy. *God! How unpleasant is this Sofia!* Roberto thought.

Finally, the girl resumed control of her appearance, which became composed and severe; they sat down at a short distance.

"Is your mother well?"

"Quite well, thanks."

"And... Lulù?"

"She's well, too."

A silence. Roberto felt a strange feeling, like a joy

that filled him with bitterness. "Is Lulù busy?" he asked.

Sofia repressed a slight movement of impatience. "She is at the ball, with our mother, at the Dolfino's," she said quickly, almost as if to avoid other questions.

So Sofia was alone, and if he didn't want to appear as the rudest of men, he would have to remain with her! Roberto had, at the thought, an irresistible wish to run away. Yet he didn't move.

"I came because at the meeting we didn't have the legal number to vote," he said, as if to apologize for his presence.

"Lulù was not expecting you... I'm sorry..."

"Oh! It doesn't matter!" Roberto interjected. The interruption was too quick, and therefore not very flattering for the absent girl. "And you," he went on, "didn't go?"

"No... You know I don't really like dancing."

"Do you prefer reading?"

"Yes, by far."

"Are you not afraid it will hurt you?"

"I have good eyes," said Sofia, raising her face to her interlocutor.

And beautiful, said Roberto to himself, and then, aloud: "I meant..."

"In the moral sense, maybe? I don't believe so; in the

books I read, I always find a great peace.”

“Do you need peace?”

“We all need it.”

Sofia’s voice was severe, resounding, and yet Roberto was pleased by it as if he was hearing it for the first time. He had the impression of being in front of a woman so far unknown, who was revealing herself to him with each of her words, each of her acts. Because Sofia had lost her coolness, she let herself look at him, smile to him, talk to him like a friend. What had been between them before? What was born now?

“When I like a book,” Roberto resumed, “I am very keen to know the author, to know if he is good, if he, too, is loved, if he, too, has suffered...”

“You might be disappointed. The authors always describe other people’s love, not theirs.”

“Out of respect, perhaps?”

“Out of jealousy, I believe. There are instances when love is the only hidden treasure of a soul.”

But Sofia’s voice did not alter, saying these words. Her face was so honest, so simple, so pure, so convinced in uttering those words, that Roberto didn’t feel any surprise, hearing her so confidently talk about love. He didn’t wonder about anything, any more, all seemed natural, foreseeable; even that night, spent alone with that singular maiden, seemed to him that had been long before decided, and long awaited. When they separated, they looked earnestly each other’s face, almost trying to recognize themselves. Sofia handed her hand, Roberto took it and bowed; a door closed heavily. They were divided.

Beyond the charm in the presence and conversation of Sofia, Roberto felt his mind in chaos, his brain in shambles. He was at once cheerful, melancholy, he wanted to die and was full of life; he no longer knew what to think about Lulù, about himself, and about the future.

Sofia was very, very happy! That's why she was sobbing, her head sunk in her pillow.

IV.

Three months had passed, and Lulù's marriage kept being delayed. Sometimes her mother, who didn't quite understand these delays, called her daughter and asked her about them.

"I want to wait," Lulù always answered. "I need to know Roberto better."

In fact, the girl had become quite an observer. She went around as usual—as usual she sang, laughed, joked, but often interrupted these pleasurable occupations to investigate her sister's behavior, or to listen to every word Roberto spoke. She was often seen with her lips tight, eyebrows frowning, deep in concentration. Now Lulù looked very much around herself.

And strange things took place around her. Roberto was no longer serene and joking as usual, but pensive, pale, and troubled. He spoke little, was distracted: Many things that he used to find interesting now had become uninteresting to him; sometimes, with great effort, he managed to control himself and return to the former self, but only for a short time. He was not used to concealing, he had never done it, and he was bad at it: His passions, his internal troubles, were apparent to anyone's eyes.

Another Sofia had emerged; that is, a restless and nervous Sofia, who sometimes embraced her sister with effusion, sometimes spent a long time without seeing, indeed, fleeing her. Sudden blushes passed over her face, feverish redness; there was a flame on her eyes; her voice was now deep and uncertain, now shrill and dry; her lips were often trembling; her hands shaken by an imperceptible tremor. She could not sleep at night: Lulù used to get up, barefoot, to listen at her sister's bedroom door, and heard Sofia agitated and weeping. When asked about it, Sofia replied that she was fine, she was always the same.

When Roberto and Sofia were together—and it happened almost every day—their change appeared even clearer. Few words, answers too quick or too vague, strange looks; for entire evenings they would not talk, but one was studying the movements of the other. They never sat next to each other, but Roberto always found the way to pick up the sewing work or the book that Sofia had touched. Sometimes she didn't appear in the room and Roberto, more and more restless, stared at the closed door, answering distractedly to the conversation around him. Sometimes, five minutes after Sofia appeared, he picked up his hat and left. The girl was becoming more and more pale, black circles formed beneath her eyes; she decided not to be seen anymore. She closed herself each night for eight days in her room, trembling with impatience, suffocating her laments.

One evening Lulù entered the room. "Can you do me a favor?" she asked Sofia.

"What would you like?"

"I need to write a note. Roberto is alone, out on the terrace. Go keep him company."

"But I..."

"Do you want to keep staying closed up here? Does it cost you so much to do what I ask?"

"Will you come soon, at least?"

"Just the time to write a few lines."

Sofia started toward the terrace, trying to steel her heart for those few minutes.

She stopped at the threshold. Roberto was walking; she approached him. "Lulù sends me," she said in a low voice.

"Were you forced to come?"

"Forced... no."

She was trembling all over. Roberto was close to her, his face overwhelmed by passion. "What have I done to you, Sofia?"

"Nothing, you did nothing to me. Don't look at me like this..." she begged, dismayed.

"Then you know, Sofia, that I love you so much?"

"Oh! Shush, Roberto, for God's sake! What if Lulù heard us?"

"I don't love Lulù. I love you, Sofia."

"It's a betrayal!"

"I know, but I love you. I will leave..."

"Well," cried Lulù from afar, appearing from another door. "Well, did you make peace?"

But no one answered. Sofia ran away, hiding her face in her hands, and Roberto remained motionless, silent, suddenly numb.

"Roberto!" Lulù called out.

"Miss."

"So, what happened?"

"Nothing: I am leaving."

And without even saying goodbye, he left with a desperate gesture. Lulù's gaze followed him and remained thoughtful.

"One went in one direction... the other, in the opposite direction..." she murmured. "And what happened before? Enough, I'll have to put myself to work!"

V.

"...So, for all these very good reasons, I can't marry Roberto Montefranco," Lulù said to her mother.

"They are absurd reasons, my girl," replied her mother, shaking her head.

"Well, I'll be very clear then. I don't like Roberto, and I am not marrying him!"

"At least now you are honest; but it's still a passing whim. Roberto loves you."

"He will console himself."

"You gave your word."

"I am taking it back. We are no longer in the times of forced marriages."

"What will the world say?"

"Mother, can you define the world?"

"The people!"

"Who are the people? I don't know them; I am not obliged to be unhappy for the sake of the people."

"You're an awful girl! How should I fix this with Roberto? What should I tell him?"

"Whatever you want. Mothers are made for this."

"Yeah, to fix your messes and faults. There will be a scandal."

"I don't believe so; you will tell him kindly, politely. In fact, I give you permission of talking badly about me, to say that I am capricious, flighty, lazy; I would add that I would have been a poor wife, that I am not serious, that I have no dignity, that my sister is..."

"Your sister? Did you take leave of your senses, Lulù?"

"Ah! That's a very good possibility. For now, Roberto and Sofia are indifferent to each other, but when they will get to know each other better, they will appreciate each other... and then... who knows, who knows! You would have the praise of being a good mother, marrying your eldest daughter first..."

"Indeed..."

"I won't lack other husbands, I'm only eighteen, and I want to have fun, I still want to dance, I want to enjoy my youth; with my good little mummy..."

"You're a little devil," said her mother, moved, embracing her daughter.

"So we agree? We give Roberto the bad news, but we add that we want to remains friends, that we always want to see him. If those two have to love each other, they will: let Fate decide."

"But do you think, Lulù, that things will be fine? You know that I don't like tangles."

"Oh, Mother, you are so difficult! You are worse than St. Thomas! Yes, yes, I assure you, with my proven experience, that there won't be scandals. Roberto is ultimately a gentleman, and will not insist that I marry him without loving him."

"What I find impossible to believe is this business with Sofia..."

"Nothing is more possible than the impossible," Lulù replied gravely.

"Oh dear, you and your axioms! Come on. Let's let time do its job; perhaps it will govern our affairs. That doesn't mean that you are not a bit crazy."

"And a capricious..."

"And stubborn, lacking good sense..."

"And shrewish. I am all you want, let's hear the sermon, I deserve it. Come on: Do you have nothing to say? I am waiting."

"Give me a kiss and go to bed. Good night, baby girl."

"Thank you, Mom. Good night."

"Better this way," the good mother told herself. "Better this way. Lulù is still too young. Every day we see the sad consequences of convenience marriages. God forbid! Better this way."

"Finally!" Lulù exclaimed, catching her breath. "What a diplomacy I had to use, how difficult it was to convince Mother! I would be a perfect ambassador. What a triumph! A lot more than a triumph of love! This is the triumph of Lulù!"

She stopped in front of her sister's door and listened. Every so often, she could hear a repressed sigh: Poor Sofia had lost her serenity.

"Sleep, Sofia, sleep," Lulu murmured softly kissing the lock, almost as if kissing her sister's forehead. "Be quiet and rest. I worked for you tonight."

And the generous girl fell asleep, happy and content for the happiness of the people she loved.

***

Time, good old time, the eternal and judicious gentleman, did its job. Lulù asks herself if a young lady accompanying her sister, the bride, should wear a blue silk dress, or just a light yellow dress with simple lace. She wants to know from Roberto if there will be many cakes, and from Sofia if she will give her as a gift that nice embroidered handkerchief that looks like a puff, a cloud. Those two, who have known what the girl's heart is capable of, smile at her gay carelessness, and love her, and consider her as their Providence!

"Because I always believed," says Roberto Montefranco to a friend, speaking of his marriage, "that the spouses must have opposite natures. The extremes touch. So they will understand each other, they will merge, they will make a whole—while those of equal inclinations, look like two parallel lines: They walk together, but they never meet And in any case, when there is love...! I always said so."

SALON COMEDIES

Countess Flavia Andorno was nice, she was twenty-eight, she had a dowry of forty thousand lire, and she would not take a husband. Once in a while, she refused one. Countess Flavia read a lot, invented the fashion that elegant ladies imitated, didn't go to first performances, but to the second ones, didn't love poetry, didn't use makeup, was never ill, traveled very often, accepted courtship up to a certain limit, never spoke about politics, loved men's conversation more than women's, had gray eyes, brown skin and brown hair. She was therefore called, wrongly or rightly—I do not put my mouth in it—a woman of spirit.

For the Marquis Ernesto Carafa, the same thing: He was thirty-two years old, a beautiful head with a blondish mane, an aristocratic blond beard, an annuity of sixty thousand lire, and no trace of a wife. He courted with a certain nonchalant grace all the ladies, he danced when the others played, he didn't cultivate the *ballerina* genre, he always drove his horses himself, he didn't wear flowers in his buttonhole, didn't protect the fine arts, didn't like music, lent money to his close friends, didn't aspire to be a deputy, loved mountains like a Platonic climber, had no literary tendencies, never wrote love letters, was always in love and never in love.

Rightly or wrongly, Ernesto Carafa was called a man of spirit.

These two exceptional beings began to know each other naturally as everyone does. Then some of Flavia's girlfriends said to her: "That Carafa is really a man of spirit, why don't you have him introduced to you?" And Ernesto's friends said: "Do you know Countess Adorno? A woman of spirit, my dear fellow." And this happened three, four, twenty times, so that Flavia was annoyed, and Ernesto was annoyed. They saw each other during a walk and looked at each other with an ill-concealed curiosity, like two rare animals; but the Countess didn't see anything extraordinary and the Marquis shrugged, for the same reason. One evening, at the San Carlo Theater, a friend introduced the Marquis to the Countess's table. Few words were exchanged of the simplest kind, those that are not in the vocabulary of the people of spirit. Ernesto left immediately, smiling ironically about the usurped fames and Flavia asked herself if she had to add a name to the category of useless and foolish beings, already so long among her acquaintances. So whenever they met, a little bit everywhere, the theater, the clubs, parties, walks, they exchanged a sort of disdainful greeting, without trying to get closer or to get to know each other better.

But Fate, that, far from being a person of spirit, has perfectly stupid estimations, made them meet and forced them to stay close to each other, at the wedding of Flavia's cousin to a friend of Ernesto's. They resigned themselves to bear each other's company. Each thought to support their reputation well, so as not to look any less, and then there was a conversation with paradoxes, bizarre questions, original answers, stupendous absurdities, a firework that ended up frazzling the two pyrotechnics, leaving them in a state of nervousness, unusual for them.

"What a witty and unpleasant man! But I held my own," Flavia said when she was alone.

"An annoying and witty woman, but I haven't been left behind," the Marquis murmured on his part.

Yet the Marquis went with a certain frequency to the Countess's house and the Countess welcomed him with polite cordiality. Both were aware that the people around were pleased with this relationship that gathered the man and woman of the greatest spirit in the city: They had noticed the smiles, the curious attention with which they tried to take part in their talks, the haste with which was spread a bon mot told by Flavia to Ernesto or vice versa; finally they realized that they were treated by the public as famous actors. Were they conscious of playing a part or were they sincere? Here is the dark point that I will not illuminate. But it is sure that the play went on, recited strongly and with great interest. Belonging to the small class of the people of spirit, the two tried to do the opposite of what the whole world did. Ernesto had at first declared that he would never, ever, court the Countess and the Countess had added that she forbade him to fall in love with her, which is in fact the opposite of courting. Ernesto never sent flowers to Flavia, and she never asked for his confidences, as is common among friends. The Marquis never felt obliged to praise the hairstyle, her eyes, the arms of the Countess, and the Countess avoided talking with about him with her girlfriends. On the subject of love they agreed, they said good and bad things equally, barely touching the subject, naturally making fun of it. The same thing happened on the subject of marriage. They never grew soft, they were never melancholy or thoughtful. They were always afraid of being too sentimental, as most people are. They never ventured into artistic discussions, never talked about poetry. All the clichés, the conventionalisms, the maxims, the classic quotations, the poetic quotations, the journalistic expressions, those that the whole world repeats, because the whole world began to tell them, were banned. I say nothing about proverbs: They were strictly forbidden. For a while, they had a good time quoting them upside down at the cost of making the great Solomon and all the others who were proverb collectors shudder, but such a joke soon became very tiresome and they let it go. The Marquis was always on guard, fearing to see a mocking smile on the beautiful Countess's mouth, for some involuntary offense he made to the spirit; and vice versa, the Countess was mindful of her words, blushing if she was caught in a moment of weakness, in which she resembled too much another woman.

But in the effort of safeguarding too much their reputation, Flavia and Ernesto began to get a little boring. That is to say, not for themselves, but for the people who frequented them. People of spirit naturally have many needs. It is natural that they live a life different from the common life of the multitude. For example, when they met at a ball, Ernesto greeted the Countess and talked with her for a moment, made a little trip and went back to tell her something, without ever stopping too long, but often coming back. Around him, people were saying he had reasons to do so, as she alone could understand him. They often danced together, for the same reason, and the other admirers of the witty Countess were disappointed, hoping in vain for a mazurka or quadrille. When Flavia left, the Marquis wandered a little more through the rooms, looking bored, and then put on his coat and left too, because he didn't have anyone else to talk to. At the theater, Ernesto remained more than usual in his box, as it is very common to pay a brief visit to the ladies. If some miserable mortal, in the form of a brunette young man, in a tailcoat, shirt open to his chest, presented himself to Countess Flavia, if this unhappy, unfortunate young man, dared to venture the usual compliments, an impertinent little laugh touched the lips of the Marquis and a sharp response came out of the rosy lips of the countess. The result was the stampede of the young man. There was a rumor that the Marquis Ernesto had courted assiduously the duchess Cesira Galbiati, a beautiful young woman, tall, with sculptural forms, large Junoesque eyes, long blond hair, a real blossoming woman, but in terms of intelligence, a goose of the naive and conscientious kind. Well, it was believed that the Countess Flavia had fired more than an epigram to the Marquis, as he immediately ceased to buzz around the *Duchessina* Cesira. Again: The Countess and the Marquis had retained the privilege of many, too many strange ideas that they never failed to put into execution. When all other couches were on the Riviera of Chiaia, Flavia asked her coachman to turn the corner of Piedigrotta and drive to Corso Vittorio Emanuele. Ernesto made a turn, went through Via Toledo and Salvator Rosa and came to meet her. In the winter season, in the heart of social entertainment, parties and dances, Flavia fled to Sorrento, and after three days Ernesto arrived there, bored of the city. At first, Flavia had a visiting day, then she canceled it, seeing that all the lady friends had one, and also because the Marquis had already mocked such days. The Marquis had lost the inveterate habit of hunting every year in Calabria. Thus, little by little, a certain isolation occurred around them; the world always confessed aloud that those two gathered all the Neapolitan spirit, but in a whisper it was said that it was better to leave those two models of the spirit to each other. Flavia and Ernesto didn't notice, and when the time came when they found themselves alone, facing each other, it seemed to them a very simple thing. The public had moved away a bit, but it is for this reason that art was invented.

***

One autumn evening, the conversation between those two languished, exhausted. Not that there was nothing more to say, but a certain sense of tiredness descended upon them. All evening their spirits had brightly shone, and the graceful witticisms, the gentle irony, the polite subtleties, the biting amiability had rained without stop. Now they were silent. The Countess stretched out a little in her armchair: She was adorable under the quiet lamplight, but the Marquis, even recognizing this truth, had the good taste not to talk about it. He fiddled with a mother-of-pearl stick.

"Marriage is a great thing," he murmured, with a false air of conviction.

"For celibates, yes," the Countess replied immediately. And she adjusted her lace. Ernesto took a book from the table, read the title and set it down again.

"Do you know what they say about us?"

"I don't know. And I don't want to know it."

"Then it is a sign that I must tell you. Many of our mutual friends are in agreement that we are people of too much spirit to ever marry."

"Ah!" said the Countess, shrugging.

"What if, to prove that we have it, we did the opposite? What do you say, Countess? It would be charming!" And he opened the newspaper *Il Pungolo* to read the news.

"Charming, in fact," she answered, looking for the fan.

In reality, they were in love up to their eyeballs, like two people of spirit who have forgotten their heart.

THE WIFE OF A GREAT MAN

Once upon a time there was a girl—alas, how many there were and how many there are!—a   girl who was supposed to placidly marry a young man. He was a good boy, a wholesaler of spirits and sugar; his good friends said that never remained in storage any of the first, and too much of the second. And by this they meant, with cold sarcasm, that he was good and stupid. Conversely, an Italian language professor had declared her a prodigy; she read novels and literary sections of literary magazines, attended scientific, historical, and poetic lectures, explained puzzles, was never absent at opening nights, participated lively in the critical and unnecessary discussions that arose from them; in short, she was a modern girl, a superior girl. It goes without saying that before becoming such, her marriage to the sugar-and-spirits merchant could seem logical, but as that superiority arrived it became an absurd proposition, because every proper superior maiden must marry an illustrious man or die a spinster. The parents, who greatly loved their little daughter, were persuaded of this deep truth and sent the boyfriend packing. He wept for an hour, despaired for three days, was melancholy for a week, and ended up marrying the daughter of a timber merchant. The story doesn't say whether they had long offspring, but the honest reader is right to suppose they did.

Meanwhile, the girl sought her illustrious man and, after a thousand difficulties, found one. Her difficulties arose not because of the scarcity of the genre—because, according to our contemporaries, we are in the era of the magnitudes—but she wanted a true, authentic, beautiful, and great man. The one she chose, as usual, was a self-made man, because a celebrity that would allow him not to rise from nothing would be a false celebrity. He had fought misery, hunger, and cold, all things that were happy companions of his youth. Just like others, he entered the room from the small door of journalism, bringing with him two opposite qualities, patience and daring, and managed to obtain a name and a place in the militant ranks. Then the events always favored him, unexpected miracles occurred to him: The publishers paid him, his books arrived to the sixth edition, critics caressed him, glory showered him for all his natural life.

He tried politics, this great snuffer of artistic intelligence, and was so lucky to get out of it alive and a winner. When one of his policies was announced, the people of the Ministry took a long, hard look at themselves, the opponents sharpened the knives in their answers, the forums crowded with listeners. He was offered an appointment, and he had the strength of character to refuse it. Honors, degrees, titles, and crosses came to him from all over: He accepted everything with Olympic serenity and remained an illustrious man, observed, studied, discussed, commented, and always applauded by the public.

How the girl managed to see him, know him, bring him home, persuade relatives, would be a long time telling: Day by day, for the word *marriage* torrents of female diplomacy are dispersed in the ocean of life. Of course it was not a simple undertaking to conquer that eternally triumphant man, because he loved himself too much to love someone else much. But the young lady was rich, beautiful, elegant. She knew his books by heart and recited some excerpts of them with a graceful smile of admiration; it was a perpetual adoration of the acts, of the words of the great man. Her parents with their adoration seemed to humbly ask for the honor of such a parentage; her family's friends worshiped him, her servants worshiped him. He was inebriated by that adulation and was moved by the show of so many good people at his feet; he came down from the throne of his greatness and granted a benevolent consent.

A deserved adoration, the bride thought. A man of genius has nothing to do with the masses of other small and common beings: He lives in a high sphere, surrounded by light. His head's proud demeanor; his natural ease of his personhood; his gaze, now fixed on the earth, now lost in the sky, but always deep; the artistically disheveled hair, the furrow of the forehead, the mystery of his smiles, the ironic curve of his lips; all reveals the race of the elect. No one else knows how to enter a salon, to bow, attract all looks, be the center of attention, dominate the whole meeting. Everything he says has a hidden meaning that sometimes escapes the profane. He often says very simple things that everyone knows, but gives them a turn of elegant originality: The smiling modesty with which he speaks of himself, the kindness with which he welcomes young beginners, that veil of contempt with which he treats his opponents, the calm with which he faces the debate and the sudden rising of the idea are all things that complete his greatness. He has the singular power to give a poetic appearance to our prosaic modern suits: His shirt looks nebulous, his gloves have a soft and indefinable color, the same tailcoat acquires artistic lines—one would want to ask if this man dines, drinks, and sleeps like the rest of mankind. How sublime he must be at the moment of inspiration! And in love! To be the wife of this man, to bear his name, to possess his heart, to share his glory: Here is truest happiness.

***

I cut some notes from the young bride's diary:

Beautiful trip. Guglielmo in Rome talked to me about Roman antiquities, in Florence about the Italian republics, in Bologna about the University, everywhere about art and aesthetics. On a honeymoon!

Guglielmo's friends will end up irritating me. They always surround him, besiege him, they don't leave him alone for one instant, and with me, if I am not mistaken, they use a compassionate tone that gets on my nerves. One, in particular, when he leaves, never fails to tell me: "I recommend you the great man." And the other day, he said in a sentimental tone, "Make him happy, madam, make him happy, because History will hold you greatly accountable for it." I wonder why History should stick its nose into such matters...

We are at home. Guglielmo has four libraries, many books that are admired by visitors, but he never reads. I thought he was studying at least five hours a day. I was wrong; he must have studied in the past.

Horrible, horrible! He wears a nightcap with a pink bow, on the pretext of keeping the curl of his hair!

He would spend hours on his toilette, and this arose my curiosity, provided that husband and wife are the same thing, there is no indiscretion to see what the other half of oneself is doing. I looked through the keyhole. He studies himself in front of the mirror: I have seen him try a dozen smiles and eight different poses...

In his moments of inspiration my husband resembles a fool. And woe if you enter his room in those moments! He is rude, impolite, and shoos you away with such words...

He wants to dine with the best food. He always wants big pieces of bloody meat, which give him the air of a cannibal ripping up a Christian. Tell me again about the poet's ambrosia?

It's been eight days that my husband walks around the house, declaiming a speech that supposedly he will improvise in the House. I won't go to hear him; I can almost declaim that speech myself, I have heard it so many times.

My husband's secretary...

This blessed politics forces me to do a lot of things I don't like. I am now obliged to visit Mrs. Zeta, a kind, small woman, in fact, too kind; oh, I should cut my tongue! I know, we are weak beings, but at least we should keep up appearances! And she is the wife of a politician! Has she learned nothing at her husband's school?

I am furious: Guglielmo receives love letters from unknown ladies who love him for his books; when I made a scene about this, he replied, with his usual coldness: "My dear, marrying me you should have known it, these are the drawbacks of your position!" Call them *drawbacks*! One of these shameless women writes: *I'm sure your wife doesn't understand your greatness.* I wish this lady could see him with his nightcap!

My wife's secretary...

Guglielmo is relentlessly courting the Ambassador's wife. If you give him any grief about it, he replies that he does it for political reasons. Indeed, a few days ago, he recommended that I let myself be courted by her husband, the Ambassador: this way, the powers remain in balance and peace in Europe is ensured. Not that I am sorry to put in my list the Ambassador as well—but he is so boring, so boring...

Guglielmo can't come with me to the baths. He has to go on a diplomatic trip, where I can't accompany him. Oh well, I'll have to resign to that.

Great men: admire them... yes. Marry them, never...

A QUESTION OF STYLE

All wrapped in her otter fur, with her black hat and veil still lowered over her eyes, her hands deep in her muff, Donna Livia, standing before the fireplace, warmed her cold numbed feet to the blaze. Suddenly, in the shadows of the looming evening, she saw something white beside her.

"Who is it?" she said, recoiling, suddenly frightened,

"It's me, Livia, don't be afraid," her husband replied calmly.

"Ah! It's you, Riccardo? I didn't hear you coming in," and her voice had softened immediately, had become tender.

"I don't understand why they didn't bring the lamps."

"I just came back from Villa Borghese," she murmured wearily. Then, feeling her way, she found the electric bell on the wall and pushed the button. A servant came in with two lamps covered with blue silk lampshades that suffused the light. The sitting room appeared very dull, with its colors of slightly sad olive velvet and old gold brocade; a quantity of thea roses climbed from porcelain vases and crystal cups. Don Riccardo was wearing tailcoat, black tie, and a gardenia in his buttonhole.

"Already dressed?" Donna Livia asked.

"I had the time wrong; it's only six. I'll wait." And he lay down in the armchair, near the fire, crossing his legs. "We can smoke here, Livia, can't we?"

"Sure. Look for cigarettes; they are on that little table."

"I have some, too."

"Mine will be better, Riccardo."

"Who gave them to you?"

"Guido Caracciolo brought them from Constantinople."

She handed him the matches, waiting for him to light the cigarette.

He stretched out again, smoking.

"So, is this dinner at the Club to benefit your foundation at seven o'clock?"

"Yes, dear Livia, at seven. A dinner for men only: It will be very boring."

"Oh! Incredibly boring." Donna Livia slowly unbuttoned her black kid gloves. "I hope at least you'll have fun neighbors at the table, for you'd be less bored, my dear Riccardo."

"I'll have Mario Torresparda and Filippo Ventimilla as my neighbors."

"That Villa Borghese is an icehouse," she murmured, shivering from the cold, warming her hands to the flames.

"You shouldn't go there, then," replied her husband with his perfect serenity that nothing could disturb.

"You know... the habit. Oh, there were a lot of people. It was a day of celebration, many new faces besides the usual ones. The queen had a pale pink feather on her black velvet hat. Do you think I would look good in pale pink, Riccardo?"

"Everything looks good on you, my dear!"

"Good answer! In short, I met Maria, Clara, Margherita, Teresa, Vittoria; Giorgio was alone on his phaeton; Paola asked me if we will see each other tonight, and I answered yes. Are you coming?"

"Yes, after dinner."

"Good boy! I remained too long at Villa Borghese; I didn't realize it was getting dark, and anyway, I knew I would have to dine alone. You are so thoughtless! I also was at Sofia's, before going to Villa Borghese; oh, if you knew how many things I did today, since three o'clock! Poor Sofia, her child is always sick and has become thin, yellow; tomorrow they will wrap him up in shawls, put him in a closed carriage, and take him to Tivoli. Who knows, the change of air could be good for him..."

"Is Federico leaving with Sofia?"

"No, but he'll go to Tivoli every day. What a cold and unpleasant man! He hasn't spent a single night watching over his child, and Sofia hasn't slept for twelve nights…"

"They say it's not his, that child," said Don Riccardo, shaking the ashes of his cigarette in the ashtray.

"They say that, it's true. Sofia compromised herself too much with Guido. I met him, Guido, in Piazza di Spagna, while I was going to see my dressmaker. I went to see this dressmaker, too, for the gray dress. But it's useless, no matter how much effort she puts in it, and how much of my time she wastes, it doesn't seem to fit me properly. A dress is like a painting. When it's wrong, you can't fix it anymore, and you have to throw it away and make another one."

"You seem unhappy about your dressmaker lately. Why don't you change her? Why don't you have all your dresses come from Paris? I don't understand."

"You're right, but how should I do it? This woman has been recommended to me, and often from Paris they send concoctions of color that are impossible. Would you believe that they sent a green dress to Giulia! She was crying today. I also was at her house for a minute, to see this dress she was waiting for with some anxiety. A fiasco, my dear Riccardo, a true fiasco! A light green dress!"

Her laughter echoed around the room; then, having taken off her hat and unbuttoned her fur, she too stretched out on an armchair, on the other side of the fireplace.

Now the nervous fickleness with which she had talked was quieting down. She slowly ran her fingers through her wavy blond hair as if to smooth it.

Don Riccardo lit another cigarette, and looking at the fire, he said, "Livia, today you went out at three with your carriage. You immediately went to Sofia's, where you remained until three twenty; from there, you went to Giulia's, where you stayed ten minutes; at four o'clock, you were in front of the door of your dressmaker in Piazza di Spagna; you entered there and you immediately exited through the little door that leads to Piazza Mignanelli. You hired a closed carriage marked with the number 522. You went to Via Cesarini, number 170, first floor, in which Mario Torresparda has an apartment where he receives the ladies of the high society who are pleased to visit him. His legal residence, where he receives his friends and tarts, is elsewhere. You remained there from ten minutes after four until five fifty; you came down the stairs, and your hired carriage brought you back to Piazza Mignanelli. You didn't have change, because you can't ever think of everything; you gave ten lire to the coachman, then you immediately came out of the large door of Piazza di Spagna, you mounted on your carriage, which in twenty minutes brought you to Villa Borghese, from where you came directly here."

She had slipped on the carpet and was stretching out her arms, murmuring, "Forgive me, forgive me, it was the first time!"

"I know it was the first time. Mario Torresparda has been courting you since July, when you were in Livorno; it all began on a night of full moon. It was nothing, at first, a joke. Then from Switzerland—where he was—to Sabbina—where you were—he wrote to you. Often at first, and then every day. You have always answered—between letters and cards, there were fifty-two to fifty-five. Here you have seen each other twice: at the Pincio, in the morning, on Friday, November eighteenth, and on Sunday the twenty-eighth. Since then, you promised to go to him, but you've already broken your promise twice, Monday and Thursday of last week. Today you finally went there for the first time."

"Oh, Riccardo, Riccardo!" Donna Livia sobbed like a child. "Why don't you kill me instead of telling me these things?"

"No, my dear, I'm not in the habit of killing anyone, and I don't want to start now. Husbands who kill their wives are only found in the novels and plays of Ohnet. I am not of this opinion. I have certain ideas about honor that I find useless to submit to you, because you wouldn't understand them. Blood? No. It's not worth it, my dear. We loved each other, before and after our marriage, for a long time. Then you didn't love me anymore, as is perfectly natural, and of course you loved another. Don't speak to me of struggle, of battle, of blinding, of contrasted passion. It won't help; I don't believe in any of it. Love ends, and it's logical that this happens. Yours, for me, lasted long enough, I believe. I don't complain, as you see. You didn't do anything strange. Indeed, thanks to that long feminine habit, to that tradition to which you women always adhere, to that refined taste that makes you so seductive, you have chosen my good friend Mario Torresparda. I care for

Mario Torresparda, and I still care for him. I will not fight a duel with him, just to give pleasure to you and the public. Do you want to tell me that he seduced you? No, my dear, it's not true. Perhaps you believe it is so, on your part, and you are in good faith, but don't hold any illusions. It is the women who always begin the seduction, and the man lets himself be seduced. What fault has Mario Torresparda? None. He found a woman who was flirting with him, he allowed himself get mixed up in it, poor man, and he fell in love. I pity him. Being the lover of a married woman is not very pleasant. It's a position full of annoyances."

"Oh, how you're right to despise me!" she sobbed.

"No darling. I have no feelings for you. I took the trouble of being informed of your love to know the truth, for a simple need of determining our clear positions. Now, for the future, do what you like, I won't even take the trouble of finding out. I warn you, however, that Mario Torresparda is truly in love with you, and making fun of him wouldn't be human. Goodbye—it's seven o'clock. I'm going to dinner; enjoy your meal."

"Will you ever forgive me?" she cried out, grabbing him by the arm.

"Forgive you? There is no need for it. I find, as a general rule, that we men are wrong to take you seriously and to marry you accordingly. If this is a rudeness, I'm very sorry, but I have to go. It's seven o'clock. I'll come to Paola later, to get you. Good evening."

"Dinner is ready," said the servant as he entered.

Donna Livia, sitting on the carpet, looking at the dying fire, thought about how her husband Don Riccardo had much more style than Mario Torresparda.

A STRANGER

In the darkness of the night, the fire in the fireplace lit the room. Every now and then, a white hand assumed the color of the flames, slowly stirring up the cinders. The three girls were silent, lost in thought. All of them imagined herself to be alone, in a vague and undefined environment, with no notions of space or time. While the twilight enveloped them, they had felt the need to be quiet, to gather together. One of them, laying on the armchair, with her head resting on the back and her eyes closed, seemed to be asleep; another, all wrapped up in a shawl, curled up in the armchair, had her head lowered on her chest; the third one, with her feet resting on the andirons, was bending periodically to poke the fire. You couldn't see if they were blond, brunette, beautiful, ugly, sturdy, sick: Nothing could be seen, except the lower part of their skirts, tinged with false colors in the light of the fireplace. All traces of age, condition, and name had disappeared. They were shadows in the shadows.

After an hour of silence one of them spoke. She wasn't addressing anyone in particular. She spoke to the darkness. She had a weak voice, occasionally softened by a vein of tenderness.

"He loves me. I met him in a children's hospital, a place full of marble and children's smiles. In its serene church, ladies, gentlemen, youngsters prayed. Two children took their first communion. He had bowed his head. I don't know if he was praying, but staring at him, I saw his lips were moving. His blond and seraphic head, in that reverent act, became even more angelic. He looked at me with his blue eyes, of a light enamel blue; I felt enveloped by the sweetness of that look. What we were doing was not a sin. I prayed to the God in whom he believed. We allowed ourselves to be drowned in the same divine love. When the Mass was over, he kneeled deeply in front of the altar, then bowed to me, and he left. After, on the day of Our Lady, on a bright and beautiful day, I received at home a bouquet of lilies, a wonder of candor. I sent him my sandalwood rosary, whose grains let a mystical perfume when rubbed by the fingers. We always see each other, on Sundays, at Vespers in the church of the Gerolomini Frairs. He waits for me at the door and with trembling fingers offers me the holy water; together we make the sign of the cross. He sits a little far from me, but we often look at each other. God is certainly not offended by this love. It is pure. I read first the prayer of adoration, a true poetic hymn, and then I pass the book to him to read. We leave together; we don't talk to each other. He accompanies me home, without offering his arm. He barely shakes my hand in leaving. Every day he writes to me sublime letters, of entirely spiritual poetry, luminous essence, soulful brightness. In truth, his spirit captives in matter such a ray of ideality escapes that I feel in it vivified and warmed. I answer to his letters every day. I try to put in my words the same loving quiver, the same iridescent vibration that he conveys in his. We love each other because we love the same things; the skies of the autumn nights, the steel waters of the lakes that flicker under the pure ray of the moon, the marbles of the churches, the cold and hard floors where the kneeling knees do penance. We love each other in the cold tears that calm the nerves and dampen the ardor of the cheeks, in the slow and placid smiles that we address to everything around us, in the celestial poets like Chateaubriand, Lamartine, Manzoni, in the calm detachment from every earthly matter, in our aspirations toward what is higher than us…"

Her voice stopped, muffled in a subdued and overwhelming enthusiasm. Nobody answered her. Only shortly thereafter, the second woman, whose head was lowered on her chest, rose up and spoke jerkily, in a voice of varying tones, now too loud, now jarring and nervous, "He loves me; I love him. I don't know how, I don't know why. He is beautiful, of a warm, tawny, manly, young beauty. His hair falls on his forehead, mighty like a lion's mane. His brown eyes are fascinating. At the theater he always looked at me. Through the eyeglass lens I could feel his gaze touching me and hugging me, leaving the stigmata of passion on my face, on my neck, on my arms. I believe I gave in to a sort of magnetism, because while my head weighed as if covered with lead, my heart was expanding precipitously under the impact of blood. I kissed my handkerchief. He saw me, and a triumphant pallor spread on his face. On the staircase, he waited for me. I passed by, and he dared to shake my bare hand, to steal my glove. He spent the night under my window: I, at the window. It was snowing; we couldn't feel the cold. Since then, this life of mine has become a storm of desires, of defeats, of acute pains, of dying joys. When I don't see him, the hours go by very slowly, my desire to see him again is so intense. When we meet, we stand facing each other, pale, our hearts in turmoil, our hands burning, our voices strangled. This is the rush of love that drives us mad. His letters are short, with sentences sharp like a knife's strike, where you feel the blood of life, the excitement of nerves, the furious outburst of a supreme love. I love him as he loves me. We are both tortured by love, we both suffer the pains of the damned for the jealousy that gnaws us; both of us are drunk with love and pain, are rolling down a steep slope with nothing to grasp, to stop us. We have the same crazy and sick inclinations for the red flowers of the poppy, for gloomy and tragic things, for flaming sunsets, for fiery dawns, for the deep sea blue, for the malaria-infested plains cooked by the sun, for strong perfumes, for inlaid gold that seems to flow, fluid, liquid, on the black background of the lacquer, for the exhausted crickets dying of love in the fuming furrow, for the black moths burning around the lamp. We love each other: He is my poet, and I am his goddess. With me, for me, his pours his few, hot tears; with him, for him, I find my dissolute, inebriating smile. We understand that we live for one thing only—love, and that for thing only we will die—love. Ours are the throbbings, the pangs; the tremors in the slight shaking of a hand, the incontrollable pallor, the desperate quivers. He destroys my life; I destroy his..."

Abruptly she stopped, clutching her face with her hands. Thus the third spoke, quietly, with a controlled, monotonous voice. "He loves me; I love him. At least, every now and then, so I tell myself. At least, every now and then, I believe I love him. We are not at all sure of it. He never believed in love: I don't believe in it, from the moment he destroyed my faith. A heavy day in an academy room, while a mad speaker tried in vain to infuse his false enthusiasm in the audience, he said to me, 'All of this is very ridiculous.'

"'Very much so,' I replied. He bowed, satisfied that he had found a woman that was cynical like him. He never wrote, never writes love letters to me; I don't write them to him. We don't believe in love letters. He never gave me a strand of hair, nor a ring, not even the smallest gift. He told me that all this stuff is useless, that it always ends up in the trash. When I tell him that I love him, he smiles in disbelief, and answers, 'Well, don't bother to tell me, for I don't believe you.' When I swear to him that I love him, he lets me talk, then he says, smiling, 'Don't swear, don't swear. You know nothing; it may well be that you don't love me.' He doesn't turn pale, doesn't blush, doesn't try to visit me, doesn't try to sit next to me, doesn't shake my hand, doesn't offer me his arm. His only effusion is a smile— a cold, slow smile. He never has any enthusiasm, never gets excited for anything. He doesn't understand art, doesn't understand politics nor science, doesn't understand God. He is a constant and calm destroyer of other people's beliefs. He is the strongest apostle of skepticism. He brilliantly supports the falsity of things, the falsity of nature, of virtue, of passion. He is strong and handsome, in his gray, almost cat-like eyes, is the metallic reflection of his mineral soul. He resembles steel. It is made of one piece. Neither sighs nor tears move him. He doesn't believe them. I break myself against him. From the moment I started loving him, my soul was overcome by his influence, it changed. What he doesn't believe, I don't believe. What he wants, I do. When, in a moment of desperate rebellion, I ask him, 'Why do you love me, then?'

"'He hesitates, gets upset, and answers, 'Who knows? I don't know: We know nothing.'

"'I repeat with him, 'We know nothing.' We remain silent, pensive, lost in the boundless doubt of two parched souls...'"

Silence fell again in the room. Nobody broke it again. In the warm and dark surroundings, the echoes of the three loves, so profoundly different from each other, finally quieted down.

Yet it was the same man that those three women loved.

OVER THE TOMB

That singular artist made unique paintings. His great merit was the energy of the concept, strongly evoked through the power of color. His paintings were not admired by everybody, especially not by people who take pleasure in the detailed, colored, and completely filled canvas; especially not by the lovers of elegant and pale watercolor figures; or those who go in ecstasy before the delicate tones of an oleography. Those who had these gracious, gentle, and petty tastes found his paintings hard, too strong, too full of things. The air one would breathe in those works was too full of oxygen for their weak lungs. The painter's landscapes were always twisted and violent, with broken lines; his sunsets were tragic, almost as if violent passion lay in the blood of a rayless sun. His interiors were gloomy, without background, without concessions of form, without those artifices of style that would highlight more a carved high chair, a large fireplace rather than the characters of his painting. They would also attribute to him a certain disdain of the drawing, a bizarre way of twisting the rendering of his characters, a search for serious subjects, that make one think. His paintings had character.

The artist was still young and robust, despite eight or

ten years of continuous labor to be accepted in this society in which it seems that not everyone enjoys the right to live. He had done nothing else but work, and success had come slowly, but it had come. He was thirty-six years old, and tall, very strong, with a powerful, leonine head, a little sharp in its features, with certain Herculean shoulders that coped with any labor. When the fury of painting took him, he would remain up to twelve hours standing before the easel without feeling a moment of weariness, without turning pale. To find a landscape, he walked for hours and hours, hiking over rocks, descending into ravines, climbing trees, climbing over walls, with the stubborn idea of seeing what he had to paint. He was constant, tenacious, and relentless in his will.

At the age of thirty, he had married a small, white, slender, blond creature, almost a child, so very gentle, pretty, sweet. In reality, he, such rough and huge artist, would not have dared to ask for that blond and delicate poem. He almost felt he might break that delicate little flower. But she captivated him so much with her childish airs and the birdlike trills of her voice that he mustered the courage to ask for her. They gave her to him. He was already an excellent artist. The critics took him seriously; his paintings were sold immediately, not at a very high price, but enough to give him some nice comfort. He married his gold little button.

He was very happy at home, because Bianca, his wife, made it elegant, fragrant with the smell of flowers, warm in winter, very cool in summer for him. He knew nothing of a home stewardship, of the mortal annoyances that afflict the mind of an artist. But the deep and only love of his life was that quick young girl who walked about the house with her luminous head, her big serene and innocent eyes. He loved her as a lover, as a husband, as a brother, with a love made of protection and adoration.

It is not known whether she ever loved the artist or not. She had married him. All the praises given to her great artist had perhaps moved her to love; but after their marriage, she got used to them, and grew indifferent. Of course, like many women, she didn't understand anything about art. It seemed to her an extravagant and useless thing. When she saw her husband thoughtful, agitated, she shrugged her shoulders with a small show of disdain. She understood that paintings produced money, but people who bought them seemed to her a bit mad. When her husband would talk to her about a painting project, she would listen, hiding a yawn behind her little hand. Finally, faced with his enthusiasm of the creating artist, she would throw these worried questions, "Do you think people will like it? And will you be able to sell it?"

He was dismayed. His wife didn't understand, but he adored her. When he realized that in confiding her, his ideas annoyed her, he stopped doing it. He kept his dreams for himself. She, alone at home, began to get bored. She wanted to go out; he couldn't go with her. Horribly and silently jealous, he let her go out by herself. In front of the painting he was working on, he trembled with rage, thinking of those who would look at his wife in the street, give her a few compliments, perhaps follow her. On the canvas, the strokes of color became strong and passionate, but at home he asked nothing, made no complaints. He allowed her to receive at home once a week, like a great lady. Or rather, she gave such permission to herself, without asking. He made quick appearances on those occasions, a little distracted, embarrassed.

She, in anger to see his tie crooked or his hands dyed in color, murmured, shaking her sweet little blond head, "These artists!"

He also accompanied her to the balls. He would find himself disoriented, with his big shoulders pulling his tailcoat out of shape, with his serious face where smiles were so rare. She would remain there until dawn, dancing like only delicate little women can dance. He would watch her pass from the arms of an elegant fool to those of an ugly and bad man, full of good humor, lavishing her wits and charms to a crowd of indifferent people. But he wouldn't say anything to her, very happy when he could wrap her in her white cloak adorned with feathers and take her away. She would yawn in the carriage, dozing. If her husband gave her a shy and light kiss, she remained still, pretending she didn't notice it, so she wouldn't have to give one back.

At first she used to occasionally go to his studio, for a cheerful surprise visit, and he would feel blessed with these visits that seemed to light up with love that gloomy room. But the staircase was steep, she got tired, and stopped going. The long hours of work were passing so slowly; she never came to make them seem shorter. That strong man, that great artist, bent his head and thought.

One day, no one knows exactly when, the artist's

wife took a lover. She was almost always alone, unemployed, neglected because of those four spans of painted canvas, so she used to say. And these great artists are not capable of being good husbands, she would add. And she betrayed him without qualms. The lover came to the house, like many others, sat at the family table, took an interest in things at home. Her husband had no suspicions. He would shake hands in a friendly manner with the man who was stealing his wife. Everyone knew it, except him. It is the rule; it's in the order of things. He, truly lonely, truly abandoned, had instinctively painted beautiful paintings. One of which was indeed beautiful, and his wife's lover bought for twelve thousand francs. This disgrace became known; only her husband didn't hear of it.

When the husband spoke of the great quality of his painting, his wife smiled strangely, as if to say, "If Carlo didn't love me, he would never have bought his painted canvas."

Then, the husband began to notice something. His wife went out at strange hours. She had been seen entering a house where Carlo, the lover, had an aunt. The husband, in spite of his blind trust, was upset. He talked to his wife about it. She answered him haughtily. She told him she would not tolerate any criticism. He was silent. Another time, as suspicions grew, she answered crying. He was silent. Finally, when his suspicions were on the threshold of certainty, she only answered this, "If you continue to insult me, I will leave you forever, you will not see me anymore." He was silent. Never again, never again was said a word among them on this subject. He feared seeing her leave.

It was then that he made his major painting of Paolo and Francesca. The scene is dark. It is a room with walls covered in leather, without ornaments, without frills of sculpted tables or twin windows. A bed covered in black velvet is in the middle of the picture. Lying on the bed, dead, with numbed hands and the white and smiling face in contrast with the black velvet, is Francesca. Collapsed on the ground, white, dead, with his back against the bed, his head close to Francesca's, is Paolo. There is blood on Francesca's dress, blood on Paolo's fitted jacket, a pool of blood on the ground. The two heads, close together, seem to be still kissing. Lanciotto is not there, but he is everywhere. His absence is of an exceptional artistic effect. Everything is sober, everything is severe, everything is tragic—even the kiss, especially the kiss. No mimicry, no choreography. A Greek Aeschylean fatality hangs in the picture.

It was his best work. The public went wild for the artist; his wife smiled, examined carefully the painting, liked Francesca's dress, and nothing else. The painter expressed his intention not to sell the painting. But his wife's will was to sell it. And it was sold.

In the same year, the artist died of hydropsy, like so many other big men.

***

The day before yesterday, I passed by his grave. A candid, new monument full of wreaths. On the stone, in grieving verses, two names, two people are still grieving over his premature death. They are his wife and her lover—and the betrayal is still there, carved in

98

marble, under the light of the sun, under the blue skies, among the flowers; that pompous and shameless betrayal lays over the artist's bones.

HANNIBAL'S VICTORY

After a year of marriage, the Duchess Adriana di Castroreale was abandoned by her husband, who ran after Princess Natalia Lapouckine, Russian, while the Duchess was traveling across Europe. Therefore high society began to observe and asked, "Who will be the one comforting the Duchess Adriana?" But this abandonment went to the head of the beautiful lady, who had a nervous, very excitable temperament, slightly inclined to originality. She persuaded herself to be desperate, cried for two days, stayed awake for three nights, got dressed in black velvet and went out in a closed carriage. No dancing. Theater, a few concerts, some charity events, but with her dress severely closed at the neck, no flowers on her head, no jewels. Naturally, she enthusiastically decided that no one could possibly console her, and renounced love, as she had renounced diamonds. Every concealed or manifest courting, every nascent love, every furtive passion were rejected with methodical haughtiness. The most valiant tried, but one can't win a bias that is not nurtured by reason, but by stubborn fantasy. The most resounding defeat was that of Count Giorgio Filomarino, a very ugly, witty, audacious and irresistible man, who, wishing to play a daring game with her, did everything wrong, offended the Duchess and was even thrown out of her house.

After such an event, high society said, "Duchess Adriana is indifferent." And just as every philosophy dies when it has found its formula, so every woman is no longer interesting when she has been defined. Adriana passed among the characterized women: Princess Giovanna was intelligent and evil, Countess Francesca was riding too much, Princess Ester was blond and sensitive, Duchess Adriana was indifferent. She ended up among the pre-established answers, the trite sentences, the immutable definitions: She had been assigned her part, and no one thought about her any longer.

***

She, who understood all this, became proud of her own virtue, warmed herself to a chaste, severe ideal of life; she sincerely believed in the firmness of her own character, in the uniqueness of her own soul. Her friends used to tell her, "You, Adriana, who you are an indifferent woman, etc., etc." Her aunt, the Marquise of Sorito, used to say, "My niece, who is an indifferent woman, etc., etc." Her friends went so far as to tell her, "You, Duchess, who are an indifferent woman, etc., etc." In this way she became accustomed to thinking of herself, to repeat to herself, "I, who am an indifferent woman, etc., etc." Gradually her worshipers thinned out. Love was followed by homage, which caressed her vanity, but left her isolated. They would greet her with great waving of hats, she aroused a murmur of admiration, but the visits were scarce in her theater box and in her house. People respected her too much.

When a newbie started to court her, his friends were immediately ready to warn him that it was useless, that he would waste his time, and he would abandon the field even before the Duchess could dismiss him with a glacial look or a biting word. Adriana felt increasingly elated in her part of the indifferent woman, in spite of the small wounds to her self-esteem, and she felt a sort of intoxication in the sacrifices she endured.

***

But a certain Hannibal Massenzio, a strange and reasonable young man, didn't believe in any woman's indifference. If he had proof of this, it is not known; but on this point, he had strong convictions. He used to tell everybody that women end up loving, and all it took is to know how to find the moment in which they want love. When they talked about Adriana's indifference, he shrugged. Honestly unemployed as he was, he began to court her almost as a joke: She rebelled, as she was accustomed to, which served to evoke some interest in Hannibal's soul. *I would like to make this woman fall in love*, he thought to himself. Since he couldn't do it by means of assiduity, always finding in her that stern attitude of offended virtue that irritated him, he walked away, adopting the most common means by which many women let themselves be won. The Duchess only cared about him one day, asking a common friend about him. He told many people that he would marry Maria Mormile, a beautiful young woman, to see what effect this rumor had on the Duchess; and the first time she saw him, she congratulated him with nonchalance. Hannibal understood that he was dealing with a refined woman, and he dropped the usual tricks. He returned to her house. He was greeted with propriety, but without joy. Only in the depth of night, in the darkness of her room, the Duchess Adriana allowed herself to smile, flattered.

But the next day she made amends for that smile, redoubling her resolution, arming herself with the most glacial indifference. While she consoled herself on the inside, she showed herself indifferent and contemptuous on the outside. The small, daily sins of vanity she committed increasingly exacerbated the appearances of her virtue, similar in this to the passionate mystics who become most elated in the bitter pleasure of repentance. After all, she was perfectly sure of herself.

Hannibal was getting excited in that dangerous game. The Duchess Adriana would confuse him. He no longer understood the way one conquers women, he made mistake after mistake, bewildered, relentlessly stubborn like a child. Sometimes he would try to reason, to convince himself that Adriana was incapable of loving, and therefore it was better to leave her alone, if he didn't want to run the risk of falling in love for real, which would have been a great disgrace in those conditions, But he was too irritated by the behavior of that unpleasant woman to decide to retreat once for all.

Then, gradually, seeing her more often, having caught certain revelatory moments, he persuaded himself that Adriana could love, indeed that she would love when she realized what love was, when her soul had been educated to feeling, when she had lived next to love. He devoted himself to the beautiful project of this education, of this regeneration, with the enthusiastic courage of those who believe they have to fulfill a mission. The elegant leisure of his life was over; he had found how to fill his days with action and his nights with dreams. Although often whenever his sarcastic nature would take over, he would laugh at that legendary hero, at that wandering knight answering to the name of Hannibal Massenzio.

And yet in spite of his self-deprecating attitude, his courting of the Duchess became more assiduous, more complete, and more open. On the pretext of educating her to love, he sent her flowers every morning, went to see her every day at two o'clock, saw her again at five for a walk, wrote her a note after lunch, found her every night at the theater, at the ball, at the concert, at family gatherings. People were starting to pity him. But they didn't say anything to him yet, believing that the story would end soon. Instead, it lasted. Adriana opposed a lively resistance to such fierce courting, as if a perfect defense plan had been established. A few small, feeble concessions, a more languid look, a lovelier intonation in her voice, a more abandoned hand, comforted Hannibal for an instant, but these lasted only an instant. In reality, he ended up despairing.

In reality, he ended up falling in love, like all those who pretend too much to love. He wrote to Adriana letters filled with passion, to try to move that insensitive heart, and in return he received a courteous sentence, a little word of kindness, a smile that calmed him for a short time. When they were together, there was a constant struggle where the eloquence of true love ignited Hannibal's words, in which passion made him more beautiful, more seductive—a struggle where

Adriana constantly denied herself using all the subtleties of dialectic, with that infinite art of the paradoxes and axioms that women use in all sort of variations. From these struggles, Hannibal came out exhausted, weary, confused, every day wishing to run away, every day staying; but Adriana was also weaker and more scared every day. Hannibal's love at every hour pounded at her heart, asking to enter: the flowers made her romantic, the letters softened her, the warm words, the acts of despair shook her.

She wanted to harden against these impressions, but she couldn't. Pushing back, she would become cruel towards Hannibal, who, in love as he was, couldn't know, couldn't notice his progress. She raged against him, chased him away from her presence and, when she remained alone, cried. Hannibal knew nothing of these tears. Adriana lived surrounded by love, she was impregnated with love, saturated with love, daydreaming of all its sweetness, understanding the triumph of feeling. Hannibal, seeing her prouder, ruder, meaner, was more and more convinced of the hopelessness of his passion. He spent a day without seeing her, but spent the night strolling along the Chiaia Riviera; he didn't write to her for two days, but ripped up four very long letters. Then he retired for a week in his villa in Capodimonte.

"If she has even only a shadow of affection for me, she will write me a note," he thought, shutting himself in his hermitage.

***

For four days, the Duchess Adriana resisted not

having news of Hannibal. But she felt defeated, and she was only delaying the moment when the first word of love would come out of her lips. Hannibal was not visiting, and her house seemed deserted. She died of boredom at the theater. One morning she entered the church, seeking refuge in mysticism, but afterward, she found her soul more afflicted than before. At home, in her bedroom, she cried twice. She wished to die, dressed in white satin, with her hair loosened, covered with flowers. She regretted not having become a nun. She wandered through the rooms like a damned soul. A deep tenderness would rise from her heart to her lips. Finally, one evening she decided: Tonight, at midnight, I will write a note to Hannibal, he will receive it tomorrow morning. That was her resolution. While she was lying on her armchair, abandoned to her sorrow, the arrival of Count Giorgio Filomarino was announced.

"A welcome visit, he will help distract me," she thought.

Count Filomarino had recently been welcomed again at the Castroreale residence. The Duchess had kindly decided to forget his past romantic advances, especially as the Count returned just as a friend. Indeed, they said that he was addressing elsewhere his affections, and in fact, he was happy every time he met Hannibal at the Duchess'. He was harmless, in short. That evening he stopped for a moment in the doorway, surprised, noticing that unusual darkness, those chairs out of place, those open books spread around, those fading flowers, the Duchess' eyes swimming in tears. Their conversation started slowly, in a low voice. From time to time, Adriana ran a hand over her forehead, as if she wanted to dispel her thoughts. They talked of simple things, of usual topics of conversation.

But two or three times Giorgio Filomarino, staring at Adriana with his dominating eyes, saw her become pale. Adriana's voice trembled unusually two or three times. Without realizing it, they started talking about their feelings, and then Giorgio was tender, delicate, imperious, melancholy, ironic, skeptical, passionate, speaking wonderfully of love, with his voice, his eyes, with the expression of his face. His words became beautiful, he made every idea brilliant and profound. Adriana listened to him, closing her eyes, as a wave of blood rose to color her pale cheeks. That evening, with quick intuition, he guessed everything, he knew how to be everything, everything Adriana wanted. And when he saw her moved, with lost eyes and quivering mouth, overcome by affection, by tenderness, by love, he dared to declare loudly, daringly, his love for her.

***

So it happened that Adriana of Castroreale fell madly in love with Giorgio Filomarino. This was Hannibal's victory.

DELFINA

Under the concentrated light of the lamp, Aunt Angiolina was reading. Every now and then, she broke off, exchanged a few words with Cecilia, and started reading again. The room remained almost entirely in the shadows; not a breath of air came through the open window. July brought stifling evenings like this. On the wide table, covered with a green tablecloth, were piles of linens, stacks piled up so high that they were falling from all sides. A large closet, at the end of the wall, was wide open—in the dim light, one could barely see its almost empty shelves. By the table, a large wooden chest, tall and light-colored, with its lid lifted, lined with yellow canvas, swallowed the linens that Cecilia was placing in it, removing them from the closet, from the table, from the chairs where they were spread. Cecilia came and went quickly, rushing on her small heels, going out, coming back, never stopping.

"Are you getting tired?" asked Aunt Angiolina, suddenly feeling a pang of remorse, raising her eyes from her novel.

"No, no."

"I didn't use to get tired either.... once upon a time..." the aunt murmured, with the melancholy pose and the drawling voice she used when she spoke of the old times.

"Oh, how happy you must have been then, aunt!"

"Happy... very much so. Mine was a marriage of love."

"And what about me?" Cecilia exclaimed, laughing. "Is mine a political marriage, perhaps? Am I perhaps the Princess of Schwarzenbourg-Augustenbourg, who marries, without knowing the Prince of Assia-Darmstadt?"

She laughed. Her round little mouth, which could hardly stay closed, with its raised upper lip, was very beautiful when she laughed. But as she looked sideways toward a balcony that remained in the shadows, she gave just a peek in that direction and remained silent, as if seized by a thought. Now she was placing her petticoats in the chest, kneeling in front of it, folding them in two, carefully arranging the pleats so that the rich flounces, the embroideries, the lace that garnished them would not be spoiled. She stopped suddenly, still kneeling, with her elbows resting on the edge of the chest, her head resting on her closed fists.

"Aunt, we didn't think of something very serious. I have a lot of short petticoats, but I have only six longer ones, and none very long. What shall I wear under the red brocade dress? If I have to go to a dance, what shall I wear?"

"Indeed...my God, you can never think of everything for the trousseau! What shall we do now?"

Aunt and niece looked at each other, worried, restless.

"What if we postpone the wedding a week?"

"No!" cried Cecilia, leaping to her feet. "I think this year I will not dance, as we'll spend the winter in the countryside. Cesare is tired of dances, so I'm tired of them too..."

"It looks like a romance, Cecilia."

"You're always reading your books, Aunt. You spoil your eyes. See, I never read any, and I find it very natural that Cesare would marry me..."

She lowered her head again and began to arrange her stockings in the chest, a thick and multicolored pile in which the color white dominated.

"Should I use some nardo essence, Aunt?" asked Cecilia, who couldn't keep quiet. "They say that it protects the silk from moths."

"Yes, it does. But it's a vulgar perfume, Cecilia. Use some ireos. You should have some."

"I'll go check."

And she ran out. Aunt Angiolina also glanced towards the balcony. She sighed, looked carefully at her hands, which she had preserved soft and white, and found them to her satisfaction. Cecilia came back, flustered. She was carrying a large bouquet of yellow roses and some long branches of climbing white jasmine. Every now and then, she sucked energetically at the index finger of her left hand, which a torn had pricked.

"I didn't find the ireos," she declared. "I went out to the balcony of the anteroom and I sacked the tea-rose bush, which was full of blossoms. Also the jasmine had bloomed, I took a few branches, but what does it matter? They will grow back."

"What will you do with all these flowers?"

"I will put all their petals in the chest. The smell of dried flowers is good. Too bad I don't have any acacias; they leave an exquisite fragrance in the linens."

She began tearing away the petals of the roses, letting them fall into the chest like a delicate rain; she threw away the bare, green stems. Then she started with the jasmines, whose petals slipped between her fingers, light and fragrant. She stopped to look at her work, smiling. Aunt Angiolina shook her head with her sentimental air. Cecilia, almost as if she had been surprised in a poetic and childish contemplation, blushed. She stood still, her eyes wandering, distracted, looking for something to do or say. Then she started working again.

"Cesare and Cecilia. Don't these names go well together?" she murmured.

"There is a fatality in the names," her aunt answered seriously.

"Again with this fatality! You put it everywhere, Aunt. It saddens me, I assure you. Listen, Aunt: I have to ask you two very serious questions of exceptional importance. Do you believe, Aunt, that when we don't have anybody over at lunch, I could come down in a dressing-gown and slippers? Do you believe that Cesare is in love with me?"

"Should I answer the first or second question?"

"They are equally interesting, but go ahead, answer the second one."

"It is trivial to quote a proverb, but this one I made myself. *Who loves well, marries soon.* How long have you known Cesare?"

"One year. He courted me for six months, he's been my boyfriend for three."

"According to mathematical calculations, Cesare is in love with you."

"I was convinced of this before I asked you, Aunt. Was Uncle Astolfo just as in love with you?"

"Oh, my dear! Uncle Astolfo was in love in a very different way. In those times, people loved each other differently. We loved each other for four years against the will of our relatives. Three times we planned to die, and everything was ready for a kidnapping, when as our plan was discovered, they ended up giving their permission. Love was like a novel, then."

"And now?"

"Now it is more like theater, my dear."

"And how dressed will I go down, Aunt, when we won't have people at lunch?"

The two women, with the utmost seriousness, discussed the dress, the slippers, the collar, the scarf, as they had discussed love. In the nearby street, a barrel organ played a song by Tosti, slowly, so as to make it even more melancholy than it already was. Little by little, they were silent. They listened. They lived on the second floor, and with the windows open all the sounds of a summer evening rose sharp and clear. A little boy was crying, with that sleepy wail of a child falling asleep; a cobbler was pounding on a heel, quickly. A female voice, accompanying the organ in a whisper, hummed:

I would like to die when the sun sets.

Involuntarily, Cecilia began to hum too:

When the violets sprout in the meadow,

while the soft music, the sultriness of the July evening and the weariness put her in a tender and serious mood, making her wish to cry. She had abandoned herself on chair, looking at the ceiling, her arms loose and abandoned, thinking of a number of melancholy things. From the street, the female voice continued to sing:

I would like to die... I would like to die...

Cecilia let two big tears fall down her cheeks. She felt pity for that little woman who was singing so sadly, for the organ grinder, for herself because she was about to marry, for her aunt who was a widow and read Diane de Lys. All of this didn't last long. The organ started playing *Funiculì-funiculà*.

All the sadness of Cecilia vanished. Life was

beautiful, wasn't it? And Cesare would arrive early the next day. She had to hurry up.

"Did you decide about the announcements, Cecilia?"

"Definitely. We'll leave you the list of the addresses and you will send them out."

"You're lucky, you'll avoid the wedding visits."

"And over there, in the country, do you believe that the important people of the neighboring towns, the mayors, would want to spare us this trouble? How many first ladies, how many wives of judges, how many provincial women will parade in my house! How much fun I will have, what a great lady of the manor I will be, how lovely I will be, and how many curtsies I will do!"

"You're a child, Cecilia. Marriage is a serious and dangerous thing."

"Dangerous?"

"Dangerous."

"Why, Aunt?"

"Because of it consequences."

"I don't understand."

"You know nothing..."

"...Perhaps... perhaps because of the children?"

And a lively flame ran over her face.

"Also that... but there is something else..."

"Perhaps because there are these horrible Marquises Susannas, these Princesses Albertinas, these Countesses Elenas?

"You don't know anything. Life is a romance."

"Mine is a beautiful one, Aunt."

"These are the first chapters. Be wary of love, my girl."

"I love Cesare, he loves me," she replied with great simplicity. And she looked around, in the big room, almost as if she were calling the shadow to witness that truth. Nothing had a voice, nobody answered her; but she remained quiet and satisfied, having summarized present and future.

The closet was empty. Cecilia slowly put in the chest the smaller items, the little collars, the cuffs, the bonnets, the handkerchiefs boxes. Before putting an object in its place, she looked at it, admired it, spoke to it in a low voice, almost caressed it. She was very happy, happy to have all those ornaments, white, made of soft fabric, light with lace, gentle in shape. She almost played with them, like a child with a doll's clothes.

"Will there be many people at the Town Hall, Aunt?"

"Many people."

"And the vice-mayor will tell me something very scary? Will he look scary with his scarf?"

"The vice-mayor is mostly a bored and hasty lawyer.

But the articles of the law make one think, Cecilia."

"Of course. Will the ladies wear white hats, aunt?"

"White, especially the girls."

"Short dresses, correct?"

"Short; the smallest train is considered vulgar."

"Do people usually cry at the town hall, Aunt?"

"It's optional, my dear. Mostly people prefer to cry in church."

"...Yes, in church. In church it will be a serious matter. Will there be flowers, incense? And the beautiful altar boys, blond like cherubs, with white pleated surplices? How darling all this will be!"

"And what if behind a column was a desperate lover, Cecilia? What if this lover stepped forward, cursed you, and stuck a dagger in his own chest?"

"This is in the libretto of *Lucia di Lammermoor*. It's no longer fashionable, Aunt."

They both laughed.

"Do you believe, Aunt, that my husband will be good to me? How will I make him love me? Should I be good or bad with him?"

"Dumas says one thing, George Sand another."

"And I, Aunt?"

"Put the romance in your life, child. Nothing is

accomplished without poetry."

"Where do I find this poetry? I don't know anything about it. I'm a fool; I'm desperate, Aunt. You will make me die, Aunt."

An almost childish desolation was painted on her youthful face. Aunt Angiolina was worried, as if she, too, despaired for the novel running through her imagination.

"Aunt, Aunt, where will I put the jewels?"

"In the black leather case."

"Will I now be able to wear as many rings as I like? I will have on the ring finger, one on the middle and one on the little finger; I will finally be allowed to have diamond earrings."

And Cecilia remained enraptured, with a light in her eyes. The chest was full, the table cleared, the chairs empty; everything was in order. Yet she didn't immediately close the chest, she remained staring at its cover, almost forgetful, almost trying to remember something. She gave two or three turns in the great room, searching in its dark corners. She came back and abruptly lowered the cover, closed the locks with the small keys. Her hands trembled. She went toward her aunt, pale, and with an uncertain voice, said to her: "Oh, my Aunt, my Aunt, I'm leaving tomorrow!"

In the arms of each other, they wept. They broke the embrace when the slim and graceful figure of a young woman, dressed in white wool, appeared behind them, leaving the balcony. They stood there a bit confused, a bit mortified.

"Delfina, you must find all this supremely ridiculous," Cecilia murmured.

No, she didn't answer. But from the weariness of her brown eyes, from the ironic turn of her pure mouth, from the expression of boredom that spoiled her youthful face, it was clear that she found it all supremely ridiculous.

DUET

The two friends had cordially kissed each other on the cheeks, as in the Neapolitan custom. Giovannina, the married woman, was silent, struggling a little, as if the stairs had fatigued her; Maria, the girl, held the hand of her friend in hers, smiling and murmuring, "How happy I am you came, how happy I am..."

"Yes, my pretty one," said Giovanna, lifting Maria's chin with one finger, to look at her well in the eye, "I just came back from a holiday. I stayed there too long, in that house of mine that is almost a castle... too long... I allowed myself to be overcome by melancholy..."

"Melancholy? It doesn't look like it, Giovannina. Your face reflects serenity: Your cheeks are red, your eyes shine; you don't even have those dark shadows under the eyes that are a sign of suffering."

"In fact, I am serene," Giovanna replied, slightly stretching her lips, attempting a smile, "but this is not about me, it is about you, my smiling and placid friend. I came here to know everything you've done since we saw each other last, in July. How you enjoyed yourself, how you got bored, what you said, what you thought— a long, long, long story like the ones the children ask for. I am listening, my beautiful Scheherazade."

"My dear, from July to August I was in Castellammare, from August to September in Sorrento."

"And since the first of October?"

"In Naples."

"In Naples?"

"In Naples."

The words rang sharp and clear, both in the question and in the answers. A minute of silence followed.

"And then?" Giovannina asked again, abandoning herself with voluptuous motion in her furs.

"And then what?"

"What have you done, my heart, in all these places?"

"Ah, well. In Castellammare I went to the beach, I swam, I danced a lot; in Sorrento, I went around, on foot, on horseback, in a carriage; I read a lot, I played a lot of music, I contemplated many sunsets and many starry nights; I danced again..."

"And what about here?"

"Here? The usual things."

"Nothing new, dearest creature?"

"Nothing new, my dear Giovannina."

Giovannina tried to hide an expression of spite: The girl didn't want to confess her secret.

"Tell me what you did, Giovannina," the girl asked with much cordiality.

"Oh, you know…nothing of note, not even this year. For the beach, I went to Livorno."

"Is it beautiful, Livorno?"

"Marvelous, Maria."

"…And?"

"And I'll tell you that it's too marvelous, and makes you find all the other places unbearable. There, the sea was poetically stormy, and even more beautiful when it was calm: How many times I just stayed there, admiring it!"

"With your husband?"

"Luigi? Not in your dreams. He hates the sea. Husbands always have the serious fault of hating what their wives love. Alas, Maria, how many times have I quarreled with Luigi, because of the music of Beethoven, the color of our living room, that dear Marchesa Fulvia that he can't stand! Long, sour quarrels; he is phlegmatic, I am nervous…"

"Are you not happy?"

"Happy, happy! Don't ask such things. 'They marry so well, us poor girls…'"

"Did you love Luigi?"

"You ask me if I loved him… I rather liked him. He looked very elegant in his tailcoat, he could dance the waltz like no one else, he directed the cotillion like few are able to do. And the way he courted me! It was a whirlwind: trips at breakneck speed, scenes of fierce jealousy, crying, sobs, delirium. You know, this makes an impression on girls...”

“And then?”

“Then we got married. That’s all.”

“What doest it mean?”

“It means that I no longer care about how he looks in tailcoat, because I often see him in a simple jacket. He doesn’t dance with me anymore. He married me, he no longer cries, he doesn’t quiver anymore, doesn’t go crazy anymore, he believes in my virtue, believes in my love, believes in his own omnipotence...”

“Well, isn’t this enough? Isn’t that love?”

“No, there comes a day when this isn’t enough. Faced with the placid indifference of her husband, his royal air of conquest, the woman feels irritated...”

“Marriage is peace, Giovannina.”

“No. The irritation grows when this man a slowly neglects all the means to seduce his wife, all the means to please her, all the means to be in her eyes the most beautiful, the most noble, the most intelligent, the most in love among men...”

“A wife is not a lover, Giovannina.”

“What do you know about it, quiet and unknowing girl? I know that Luigi loved me before the wedding and couldn't wait to have my love. Now he doesn't love me anymore, because he is sure he is loved."

"You are not very lenient with him, Giovannina. Love is made of indulgence."

"No, it's made of justice. Am I less beautiful, perhaps? Am I less elegant, less gracious, less amiable? No: He is the one who has changed. Since May, I have noticed a decrease in his affection. Now he is indifferent."

"You may be deceived, Giovannina. Are you sure of the equanimity of your judgment?"

"Sure? You see, I love the sea. Not being able to stay in Naples during the summer, I decide to go to Livorno. He comes reluctantly, annoyed, finding the seawater useless and the Pancaldi bath boring. The village of Ardenza doesn't move him at all. Can you imagine anything worse?"

"But why didn't you leave?"

"Letting him win?"

"Sacrifice is a small cross to bear, when someone loves."

"So I am the one who has to endure all the sacrifices? We women will always have to be examples of self-denial? We are always the ones to love, we are to bear all the annoyances, to excuse the ridiculous behavior of our husbands, to flatter ourselves that they still love us, to condone their indifference? It's too much, it's too much; it is beyond measure!"

Giovannina had slowly become more and more heated, as if no one was listening to her, as if she were talking to herself. Instead the girl listened to her attentively, looking at her with her big bright eyes full of kindness.

"It's serious, very serious," Giovannina went on, "this getting married to someone with whom we haven't had any intimacy. Dumas must have said it many times: He thought it, I felt it. My God! To have lunch, to walk, to dine, to share a house, to live all of our life with a man with whom we only have waltzed! It is comical and tragic. And finally, on a bad day, do you know what we see? Do you know the frightful discovery we make? We discover that we don't love anymore!"

"Oh!" the girl only uttered, and hid her face in her hands.

"We don't love anymore. Nothing remains in us any more, nothing resounds any more in our hearts. We only feel silence and solitude inside. In vain we try to shake this inertia, in vain we rebel against this indifference. Love is dead. And if what we once felt was a falsehood, that falsehood has disappeared. Thus all the faults of that man, of our husband, appear to us naked, ugly, hateful; everything in him repels us, everything in us repels him. Thus here we are: Melancholy, desolate, young, with a longing for feeling that is wasting miserably, we seek love elsewhere..."

"Elsewhere?"

"In another heart that could understand us. The

other man is always ready, handsome, poetic, chivalrous, fatal: No husband can stand the comparison. The other man has the halo of poetry intact, knows how to love, knows how to lose his head, he only knows, only understands passion. The woman loves this other man by logical necessity, because she doesn't love anymore, because she must love again, because the other man is the chosen one of her heart! But you, dear maiden, can imagine with what desperate passion this woman becomes attached to this other man, you can imagine with what fortitude she clings to him, who now represents for her love and guilt, pain and happiness! Imagine if this woman, who has thrown away her whole life in a day, can let another woman have this man..."

And her words drowned in her throat, out of anger, out of love, out of jealousy. Then she stood up in all her height: "Are you marrying Roberto Montefiore, Maria?" she asked briefly.

"I am marrying him, Giovanna," said the other, standing, serious and calm.

"Why?"

"Because I love him."

Their two looks, equally in love, equally desperate, met like two enemy blades.

FIRST DATE

In truth when I saw the beautiful woman passing by, white in the face, with tawny, frizzy hair like a dark flame, green and icy eyes, a red and sensual mouth like a passionate flower, a wavering body like those magnificent snakes dancing before the charmer's stick, I asked myself who she loved and what a ruinous whirlwind her love was. When I saw her passing through love—cold, deaf, indifferent, impassive, a denial of love—with her eyes raised to heaven, living peacefully and coldly in this world, but tormenting herself in prayer like a desperate being, I wondered what event had petrified that body of woman, leaving in her soul only the torture of a useless mysticism.

***

Well, in the past, despite her hateful marriage, she had been quietly virtuous for a long time. They had married her off to a wicked Duke, young, ugly, and uncouth, who was dissipating his fortune—and continued to do so—with all the bad actresses, the dancers of the small theaters, the singers of travelling operettas. He was like that, he was democratic in love— so he said. He added that he liked the antechamber more than the living room. So he refrained from courting his wife's friends, but he was the lover of the maid, the seamstress, the milliner, even the woman who came periodically to iron at the palace. This Duke's ancestors had climbed the social ladder for ten centuries, and believed that his constant, vulgar, dirty betrayal gave his wife no right of grievance. Because a man's whim—so this ducal bourgeois used to say—must be forgiven. So he was savagely jealous of his rights as a husband, jealous without being in love, jealous for his own pride. The Duchess Emma was considered the unhappiest but the most dignified of the wives: She never knew anything, she didn't welcome gossip, she never spoke against her husband, never made a scene, always smiled. Around her were the secret loves, the audacious declarations, the passions that every badly married woman inspires. She didn't notice them. The Duke, her husband, noticed them, and every evening he brutalized her, asking her if a certain man was her new lover and if she didn't mind the Duke, he'd go and slap a certain other. He knew very well that it wasn't true, but he enjoyed these abuses in which he could let out all his instincts of a servant with a noble title.

In reality, what sustained that exceptional woman was the greatest, the most gloomy feminine pride. To fall—and all women fall—is called weakness. But to her, that was cowardice. To betray—and all women end up betraying—is called flightiness. But to her, that was called dishonesty. To her that was being cowardly, being dishonest, being like everyone else, down, headlong, groping in the mud, dirty hands, dirty skirt, dirty soul. Her pride rebelled, bursting, furious against the love that would make her so. Indeed, she hated all men who surrounded her, who courted her, who wrote to her. She hated them like enemies, like people who were fierce against her, like cruel hunters. Her pride filled her heart, taking the place of any other feeling. Out of pride she endured that ignoble husband, out of pride she didn't go back to her father's house, out of pride she smiled, she didn't love, she lived. Such sentimental monstrosities do exist—and they are called vices—but they are also called virtues.

One day, this woman found a sincere, profound and secret love, like every woman meets once in her life. He didn't speak, he didn't write, he didn't follow her, he avoided her, he was serious, reserved, of absolute coldness. But he loved her with all the strength of a youthful spirit and all the impetus of a repressed passion. How did she understand this, she who despised love, she who only understood pride? Who told her the story of that lasting, ardent, and immense love, and how did she believe it, as she was so skeptical? It is unknown. Oh, psychology is a perfectly ridiculous science; it explains the minutiae and doesn't see the serious issues. It notices the details, the nuances, the changes of tone, but can't explain the main character, the thematic phrase. It skirts difficulties, it gets closer, advances, but at a certain point it stops. What happened in the silence of that soul that opened up to love is unknown. How that building of pride collapsed, how everything was destroyed, burned, purified by love, I can't tell you. You, who loved, can remember it, and you who didn't love, are unworthy to know it.

Long, harsh, and fierce was the fight between those two. He would not ask for anything, wouldn't move forward, wouldn't move, enduring, silently, a nameless sorrow, using all his strength to hide any outwardly appearance. Did he know he was loved? Perhaps, but he didn't show such knowledge. She saw everything, understood everything, abandoned herself to day by day, line by line, knowing what she was doing, seeing the precipice, indeed opening her eyes wide to see it, in love with that precipice, mad for that fall. One day they looked at each other, pale, silent, exchanging that fiery glance that draws the soul. They understood that they were walking toward each other, inexorably, against their will, against reason, against everything. Not a word, but the one heard the steps of the other, and even though they appeared to be still, they calculated the space, calculated the time.

"The day is coming, the day is coming," the Duchess murmured, gripped by a dreadful terror.

"The time comes, the time comes," he murmured, drowned in sweetness.

Insensibly and without anyone around knowing it, the day came. The Duke could be even more uncouth, even more brutal, could chase after the most vulgar women; this didn't matter. It was for love that Emma loved Luciano, not for revenge, not for retaliation. She didn't apologize, she didn't blame others; she gave herself because she wanted to give herself, because she loved, because love seemed the highest, the best thing in life. The Duchess could be cold, severe, austere to Luciano, but he didn't suffer: He loved her, he felt that he was loved, he had to be loved.

It was a Tuesday night, at a dance. Seeing each other

from afar, they felt the same sensation: The hour had come. He approached, almost to question her, raising his eyes to his face. She didn't lower hers, and quietly, in a loud voice, told him: "Sunday, at my house. At two o'clock."

A bow, a goodbye; no more.

***

Four days between Tuesday and Sunday, four long days, eternal, febrile, delirious, in which every minute the Duchess Emma regretted having promised that meeting, would decide to flee, would get dressed, then stayed, weak, wan, unable to renounce love. When she saw her husband leave for Nice—a sign of Fate—she wanted to cry out to him to stay, to save her. She wanted to cry out to him, to the savage, to that ignoble man, to that unfaithful husband. She felt disgusted, she felt an entirely physical nausea, an invincible feminine rejection—purified by her strong love. She went up and down the house, like a feverish tiger, gnawing, unable to cry, unable to sob—then falling, in exhaustion, into a sweet stupor, as if her ache would quiet down in her sleep, as if her wound didn't bleed anymore. No, it wasn't in the outer world: She couldn't see it anymore. It was in her wobbly and jittery spirit, it was inside her, it was in her heart, it was in her brain, that fickle torment that took all sort of forms, from acute pain to exquisite pleasure. Oh, the stormy night between Saturday and Sunday, the prayers to the Madonna, the desperation, the sudden abandonment, all her being that called out to Luciano and rejected him, that cursed and adored love, that winced, shuddered, shook, trembled in delirium. Then, finally, the exhaustion, the quiet wait: the surrender.

At two o'clock the sudden, painful start. He was coming. Oh love, love, love!

Two o'clock, three, seven, midnight: He didn't come. He didn't come; he didn't come. She, cold in her madness, automatically, holding her head in her hands, trying to think, suddenly made of stone, wrote him these words: "One misses the first date only because of death."

In fact, he had died. At one o'clock, in his bedroom, as he was grabbing his gloves to go out. He had a gardenia in his buttonhole. For three or four days, he had been restless, utterly agitated. A heartache, a broken vein, because they had found blood on the carpet, where he was stretched out. The Duchess read all of this in the newspaper.

***

So she doesn't love anymore. She can't love anymore. She lives, but carrying that secret tragedy. She prays, deranged by that death that seems to be a punishment from God. And perhaps more unhappy, more miserable yet, she sacrilegiously loves that dead man, and lives with the acute desire of that love, of those kisses, of that first date, of that sin that death stole from her.

IDEAL

Laura, standing by the little table, her head bowed, was seriously occupied with the many buttons of her glove. On the back of a chair hung a mantle, embroidered in gold; a large fan of red satin on one side, yellow and black on the other, lay half-open on the table. Laura was wearing a dress black brocade with an improbable train; on the triangular neckline, a bunch of red and yellow flowers were pinned; a branch of red and yellow flowers adorned her brown hair, appearing under her ear and caressing her neck.

Cesare entered silently Looked at her for a moment, thought about what he had to say, and ended up saying, "Good evening, madam."

She wasn't startled. She turned, smiled, stretched her glove and asked, "Is it you, Sanseverino?"

"Your question is odd."

"Be content with it. I spared you another that could have been impertinent."

"Countess, tonight you're a..."

"Phenomenon, am I not?"

"Of goodness. Something unexpected. You spare me an impertinence; you are lenient! Some horrible misfortune threatens me, then?"

"Who knows?"

"I prefer the impertinence, Countess. I already imagine it. You wanted to ask me, 'What are you doing here?'"

"You guess too much, Sanseverino; it is a dangerous science."

"For me alone. I come here..."

"To see me, because you're in love with me. I know the refrain."

Sanseverino went pale, despite his show of self-assurance. He nervously caressed his thin mustache. "Indeed," he said then. "But I wouldn't have said it. You wouldn't believe it, Countess, but I can be a man of spirit even with you."

"All to my credit, Sanseverino."

His eyes clouded, but his pride helped him regain an ironic smile. "All that is good and happy in my life, comes from you, Countess," he said, bowing too deeply.

"Very well, here is a gracious compliment which is the prelude to those I will soon hear in the theater."

"It's true, you are going to the theater," he said, as if recovering from a distraction. "Why are you going there?"

"To be bored among many people."

"Be bored with me, then. The proposal is selfish; I don't deny it. But I will do my best to bore you as much as the theater would. If you'd like, I'll open the piano, and I will play you the most serious and the sweetest melodies by Lohengrin that you could hear at the San Carlo Theater. I will talk with you about lace, love gossips, trips, ribbons, as you could do with your friend Evelina. I will court you foolishly, as Giorgio, Arturo, Adolfo, or Gino could do. Then, during a fake interval, I'll pretend to come myself to visit you, and I'll tell you what I would tell you..."

"I would like better what you wouldn't tell me."

"Sad things in truth," he replied with a grave tone.

There was a minute of silence. Amazingly, Countess Laura was thinking. But she soon recovered. "And what about the audience? We will miss the audience. Who will play the audience?" she asked.

"What is the audience saying about us?"

"Oh! Something very vulgar, Sanseverino. That you love me and that I don't love you."

"And is the audience giving any reason for this, beautiful Countess?"

"No, because there is none. We love without reason and we don't love also without reason. Love and indifference resemble each other."

"You utter a monstrous phrase," he said placidly.

"I'll be late for the theater," she mumbled, impatient.

"It's only nine o'clock. It's shamefully early. Someone who is twice Countess and three times Marques, like you, can't go to the theater at this time. I wouldn't dare accompany you."

"Would it be your pleasure to accompany me?" she asked, vanity flashing in her eyes.

"An immense pleasure," he murmured, understanding her evil idea, "in spite of the sigh of compassion I would provoke in your famous audience, Countess. I'm sure, you see," and his voice flickered with anger, "that people feel sorry for me."

She didn't answer. After a pause, she asked him, "Were you at the ball at the Della Mana house?"

"I was there."

"Did you wait for me in vain?" she continued, playing graciously with her fan.

"In vain."

"I sent word that I was ill. Were you worried? It wasn't true. My dress, just arrived from Paris, was a masterpiece of ugliness."

"This one you are wearing tonight is hateful."

"Do you think so? Yet you should like these flowers of passionate colors. Don't you go preaching everywhere: Love, love, passion, passion?"

"Yes, but not artificial like your flowers, Countess,

like the false color of your ribbons, like the false stone on your fan, like yourself..."

"Oh!" she said, suddenly turning towards him.

"Forgive me. I was wrong... My head is a little confused. There is a penetrating scent, here, that is upsetting me."

"That's better," she said, satisfied, waving her fan lightly.

"I was wrong, I offended you. You are not false; you are very loyal. You made no promises to me, and you kept none. From the first moment I saw you, I judged you: You remained unchanged. I congratulate you, Countess Laura: You have character. A character of indifference, of apathy, if you will, combined with a perfect measure of vanity. A nice character: I admire you."

"Do you believe that Teresa Realps will marry your cousin Mario?" she asked, repressing a small yawn.

"This marriage seems to amuse you like my inconsistencies. It would be better for you to go to the theater."

"Thank you; it is all the same to me. If you want, I'll stay here until midnight. I also enjoy myself here."

"What could make you cry, Laura?"

"You seem to be calling me by my given name," she said, slowly and coldly, looking at him steadily with her gray eyes.

"I was asking you what could make you cry, Countess Mormile."

"I don't know... I don't know... But there must be something. I'll find it."

"And will you tell me?"

"Perhaps. Would you like to see my tears?"

"I wouldn't see them," said Sanseverino, lowering his head.

"Ah!" she said, shrugging, and she got up to get her mantilla.

They descended the staircase, arm in arm, silent, without looking at each other. At the carriage door, he greeted her with a big waving of his hat. Laura smiled.

"Will you come to the theater later, Sanseverino?"

"To do what?"

"What everyone does."

"No. I'll go play cards at my club."

"Does this distract you?"

"Not at all. Everything is useless, everything. Good evening, Countess Mormile."

"Good evening, Duke Sanseverino."

***

In the September afternoon, everything was silent.

137

All through the countryside was a great silence. From time to time, the sound of a carriage passing by on the main road could be heard. On the ground floor of the villa, a couple of servants slept on the benches of the anteroom, a maid was sewing by the window, a scullery boy was silently rubbing silver in the kitchen. Countess Laura didn't like noise in the countryside. She was in her favorite salon, which was something between a salon, a porch, and a greenhouse, where the curtains abated the light, the west wind blew amiably, a small fountain refreshed the air, and the autumn flowers gave pleasure to the eye. The Countess, dressed in white cashmere, covered with white laces, adorned with white roses on her breasts and in her hair, was swaying on an American armchair.

"I meant to tell you, Sanseverino," she said with her soft, seductive voice, "that I will remain in Capodimonte until the end of October."

"So long? Yet you don't like the countryside, you have said."

"Do you think so? I don't really know if I like it now. But its peace attracts me, seduces me. The town must be horrible, burnt by the sun, corroded by dust, full of bourgeois people and noise. How hot must be over there! In the evening, when I'm here on the terrace, I can see Naples smoking like a big steam engine. And your Sorrento, how did you leave it?"

"Beautiful and elegant; your entire circle of friends is there. Everyone wonders why you are missing."

"Do you wonder as well?"

"I dare not ask anything, anymore, you know. They are your friends. They make comments, suppositions…"

"What do they say?"

"I will never repeat it."

"On the contrary, you will repeat it to me."

"By command?"

"By command."

"They say you have a lover."

"Do you believe that I have a lover?" she asked, staring at him strangely.

He felt a shiver pass through his bones and answered, "I don't believe it."

"Why?"

Sanseverino remained silent. She picked up a rose from a basket next to her, and threw it at him. He caught it and smelled it for a long while, as she watched him carefully. Had he kissed the flower or simply smelled its scent?

"Tell me, Sanseverino. While you were in Sorrento, have you often thought of Naples?"

"What do you mean, Countess?"

"Of Capodimonte?"

"Of Capodimonte?"

"I meant to say, of me." She ended in a sorrowful tone, and blushing a little.

He looked at her, surprised. But she didn't give him time to reply.

"I read the day before yesterday, a mysterious word in a mysterious book. It is the word *ideal*. Don't smile, I knew that word, but I hadn't quite understood its meaning. It is the passing cloud, is it not, the ideal? Is it the music we have in our mind? Is it the painting we see in our imagination? Is it a beloved ghost? It's all this, is it not?"

"All this and more, madam."

"Oh, my friend, you must have, and love, an ideal. Tell me what it is."

"I can't tell you."

"What? Don't you love me?" she cried, her eyes shining.

"Yes, but I will not tell you my ideal."

"Well, don't tell me, then. I know it. I guessed it: My heart became a prophet. Your ideal is a woman, a woman who loves you. Take comfort and thank the Lord. Your ideal is alive: I love you, Cesare."

"Don't joke, Laura."

"I am not joking. I love you."

"You are mistaken, perhaps."

"I am not mistaken: I love you."

He was getting more and more pale. A tremor stirred the corners of his lips. "I beg you, Laura, don't lie! Remain beautiful, wicked, seductive, but indifferent, distant, elusive! If you want me to adore you, tell me that you don't love me."

"I don't understand you, you are crazy, Cesare. I know that I love you."

"Farewell, Laura."

"You are not leaving, I hope."

"I *am* leaving. Farewell."

"Cesare, Cesare!" She threw open the door of a balcony; the bright light of the sun wounded her. She leaned over the railing and shouted, "I have been loving you for a long time, Cesare! From the very first, from the first moment..."

"So much the worse," he said, bowing his head.

And he disappeared in the street.

LOVE STORY

Fulvio bowed, took from Paola's hand the ice cream that she, smiling sweetly, handed to him, and said, looking into her eyes, "I love you."

"You shouldn't love me," she murmured quietly, continuing to smile.

"Why?"

"Because I have a husband," she replied placidly.

"It doesn't matter!"

And Fulvio's dark blue eyes flashed with passion. She stood before him, without showing any emotion, smiling still, all red in her face, the beautiful candor of her arms showing out of the black lace of the sleeves. On the black lace and on the white arms sparkled diamond bracelets: They rested on her wrists, and she took care to raise them up toward the elbow, great care, toying with the gold chains, with the very thin bangles. Irritated, Fulvio was beating his spoon on the ice cream plate.

"Go away," he murmured suddenly, stifled by anger. "You are a hateful woman, I can't stand you."

Paola dropped her head slightly, as one does in front of an incurable patient, and turned away from Fulvio. The company was clustered around the piano, where a young, pale teacher with a big tuft of black hair on his forehead accompanied a frail girl, dressed in white, who with a faint voice sang an aria by Bizet. It was an aria inspired by the Orient, a weird lullaby, sometimes full of cheerful trills, sometimes full of long sobs. Two or three ladies were feeling languid, let the ice cream in the saucer melt, fascinated by the delicate lament of the Oriental theme. Paola's husband was rocking in a chair, smoking quietly, looking with distracted eye at the slim figure of his wife, all dressed in black, all sparkling with black beads.

The fresh sea breeze came in through the four windows of that long hall. Leaning against the window, Fulvio looked at the sea, absorbed. Now Paola offered the cigarettes to the young men and ladies who dared to smoke. And the hand that held the cigarette holder was so white, so smooth, that Fulvio felt an immense tenderness.

"Forgive me," he said, raising his pleading eyes.

"My friend, I have nothing to forgive you," Paola said softly.

"I'm a brute. You're good."

"No, no," she said, and started to withdraw.

"You never linger for a moment next to me," he murmured in a teary voice.

"I can't, my friend: These gentlemen need to smoke.

Here is my husband, in need of a cigarette..."

She flew away, graceful, offered a cigarette to her husband, smiling at him. Her husband looked at her quietly, looking pleased like a man secure of his happiness, and in choosing a cigarette, he played at length with his wife's fingers. It seemed that so many things were said between them, husband and wife, so many lovely things. And they were so young, so beautiful, so well matched, that their friends regarded them with pleasure, as people look at a couple recently engaged. All alone leaning against the window, Fulvio stared at the scene and paled; he took two or three steps forward.

But, behold, she came again to him, a slim, light. "Your cigarette isn't lit: Do you need a match?"

"Aren't you afraid," he said, with clenched teeth, but with the most amiable of smiles, "aren't you afraid that I might kill your husband?"

"Your cigarette isn't lit..."

"You'll see, I'll kill him, madam."

Without saying a word, suddenly with a serious expression on her face, Paola moved away from him, slowly, as if he had hit her with a painful word. Now everyone was complimenting Miss Sofia who had sung so well *les adieux de l'hôtesse arabe*: and the fragile girl, all melancholy, smiled modestly.

"Do you like Bizet? Sofia asked Fulvio, who had approached the rest of the company.

"Bizet?" he asked dreamily.

"Yes: I asked you if you like him."

"Very much so," he murmured, distracted.

The frail and sad girl looked at him and repeated, as if to herself, the first words of the French aria:

"*Puisque rien ne t'arrête...*"

But he didn't hear, lost in his thoughts.

"*...adieu bel étranger,*" Sofia concluded in *pianissimo*.

Now around the piano, people laughed. The young master, pale, with the big tuft of black hair on his forehead, recently arrived from London, was recounting to his Neapolitan friends the obstinacy of the English misses and mistresses who wanted to learn the sorrowful Italian arias. He would mimic their grimaces and contortions in a lively way, with the enthusiasm of the Neapolitan who takes revenge of the long season of fog unwillingly endured. Everybody laughed, especially Paola's husband. Paola, standing, was waving her large fan of black satin, where a fanciful painter had drawn a lunar landscape. And Fulvio, unable to speak, looked at Paola. He looked at her with such intensity, with such ardent fixity, that she closed her eyelids, two or three times, as if moved by annoyance. But he didn't stop. He was enthralled, hypnotized, drunk on the irresistible charm of her eyes, which didn't look at him. And she, naturally, as if annoyed by the excessive light, hid her face behind her large black satin fan. Now Fulvio could see only her bust, sparkling of black beads, and her thin hand raised, grasping the black slats of the fan: a black satin sail hid Paola's face. Everyone laughed at the caricatures of the music teacher. Fulvio's eyes were full of tears. Sofia looked at him, with a slight, melancholy smile.

Suddenly the delicate sound of a mandolin came from the windows opened over the sea. All laughter stopped, and everyone stretched their ears. The sound was approaching, and the party, as if fascinated by it, crowded at the door that opened onto the terrace. The sea was black, in the black night; high up, the stars trembled over the black sky. Through the darkness of the sea, a small boat passed by, on its prow a bright red torch reflecting over the water, lighting a fire in it. On the boat someone was playing the mandolin, but you couldn't see whom it was; you could distinguish something white, like a woman's dress. And the torch, red like blood, reflected its light in the sea; the invisible mandolin moaned; the white shadow was motionless, and the boat sped up; silence had seized the happy brigade.

"It's a romantic *aria* in action," said the music teacher, breaking the silence.

"Love duet!" a young man shrieked.

"Let's not bother them," Paola said softly.

"Hey, you, on the boat!" Paola's husband shouted, as if to contradict his wife. "Good evening, good evening, have fun!"

All the company repeated: "Good evening, good evening, have fun!"

Immediately, plunging into the sea, the blood-red torch went out, the mandolin was silent, the boat drifted into darkness and silence.

"Too much pride, dear lovers!" Paola's husband cried out.

"Good for them," said Fulvio.

"Why do you envy them?" asked the music teacher. "Naples has its own beaches full of little boats, and its houses full of white dresses."

"Nor there is shortage of mandolins!" added Paola's husband.

"What do I care about the boat and the music and the white dress? Those two love each other: I envy them."

"Oh our sentimental, sentimental friend!" two or three people exclaimed.

"Love is a wonderful thing," said Fulvio, with grave conviction.

"What a discovery, by God!" cried Paola's husband.

"We must marry," said the music teacher. "Fulvio, look at he Signora Paola and her husband: We must marry."

"We must marry," Paola repeated softly.

"We must die," Fulvio murmured.

But all friends were now returning to the salon. They

were organizing for the following evening a trip on the sea, with two little boats and music. Wasn't it better to wait for the moon to come? But no, the outings at moonlight are vulgar: One can't feel any fear, one can see everything too clearly. It is better to go in the darkness of night, like that boat of lovers. This was what the ladies were saying; the gentlemen proposed to bring dinner.

On the threshold of the door, towards the terrace, Paola said to Fulvio, from a distance, "Are you also coming on the trip?"

"No, no, listen..." he said, in a muffled voice.

But she didn't go out on the terrace. Some of the ladies talked of leaving, but to keep the guests a little bit longer, Sofia began to sing the Shadow waltz, by Dinorah. People listened, standing; but the brief, friendly voice of the girl could not execute those complicated trills, those answers to the echo. She sang that waltz as if she was crying, and indeed that music, which is the crying of an illusion, seemed a sob of sweet madness.

"Give me my fan," Paola said softly to Fulvio, who was alone on the terrace.

"No, if you don't listen to me," he said, holding the fan tightly to his lips.

"Give me my fan," she repeated, firmly and gently.

"Hear me out, hear me out, I beg you, it's very serious..."

Paola stopped paying attention to him, and went back into the salon. Now the waiter was carrying glasses full of Malaga wine, where a piece of ice floated, and she moved about the room thoughtful, smiling, serene. When she had completed her rounds, naturally she remembered her other guest who was standing alone, in the shadows, on the terrace, between the darkness of the sky and of the sea.

"Give me my fan, my friend."

"Hear me out..." he said again.

And his voice was so sorrowful that she stopped. In the salon, now, the wine had cheered out everyone, and they were singing a Neapolitan song. She listened to Fulvio's words.

"Listen. I must speak to you. I must tell you some very serious things. Don't interrupt me, Paola, I beg you. Listen: I have many, many things to say to you. But I'll say them quickly, don't you doubt that. Now I can't do that. There are people there, happy people: I am very unhappy, Paola, if you don't listen to what I have to tell you. Be patient, I beg you. I am deeply suffering. You are not suffering, I know, but you are very compassionate. I have to talk to you. We must be alone. Listen. I am not leaving this terrace. Close the door, they'll think that I have left. Please, close it. Your husband will go to bed... and I want to talk to you. I'll wait out here, as long as you want. When he sleeps, come."

"I will not come," she said softly.

"Listen, Paola, I feel like dying. Over there, they sing

and laugh; here is a man in agony."

"I will not come," she repeated, calmly.

"Listen! I implore you, in the name of your conscience as an honest woman, in the name of your virtue as a girl and as a bride, of your sweetness and your pity, don't deny me this last favor."

"I will not come."

"If you won't come, I'll kill myself, Paola."

She looked at him for a minute.

"I'll kill myself, Paola, if you don't come. You are a Christian. You will not let a man die this way."

"I will come," she said.

II.

And she came. The night was deep, now, on the Neapolitan gulf, and far away, flickering stars glittered. Along the deserted road to Posillipo, which overlooked the terrace of the villa, a row of lights ran all the way to Naples. Deep solitude, deep silence. The shutters of the balcony that opened onto the terrace opened very softly and a white shadow slipped lightly towards Fulvio, who had been waiting for three hours.

"Thank you," he said, trying to see Paola's face in the dark.

"We are in grave danger of death," she replied, very gently.

"I know," he said, bowing his head.

He didn't speak. Instead, just when he had snatched from Paola her fateful promise, his passion was in a state of exaltation. In the first hour of his waiting, he had done nothing but repeat to himself, breathlessly, what he wanted to say to Paola. And certain words, certain sentences, muttered under his breath, had drowned him with emotion. She still didn't come. He heard the servants coming and going, inside the house, tidying the rooms, closing the windows. He could hear the quiet voices of Paola and her husband, talking, but he couldn't hear their words. Then everything was locked, the lights went out, and a great silence reigned. He began to tremble with impatience, not daring to move, curled up in his place, with his nerves tensed, confusingly repeating, passage by passage, what he wanted to say to Paola, as a desperate child tries in vain to remember the lesson he learned. Paola didn't come. He had counted the gas street lamps a hundred times, on the road to Posillipo: there were thirty-three, but he couldn't distinguish the others in that line of lights. To kill some time, he thought of counting the stars, but he lost himself in the sky. How many hours had passed? Was that night eternal?

And a resigned despair got hold of him, made him lose heart: Perhaps Paola would never come. All that was left for him was to throw himself into the sea. He would never let himself be found there on that terrace once the day came. And such idea, such a solution quieted him down. A deep dejection won him over, and he lost track of time and place. So much so that the opening of the balcony and the appearance of Paola's shadow barely startled him. Now he couldn't find anything to say to her anymore. Everything was over; he could throw himself in the black sea.

"What do you have to tell me, my friend?"

"That I love you."

"You already told me. Nothing else?" And she started to leave.

"I love you, I love you, I love you!"

"My dear friend, my husband is next door, sleeping. If a mosquito whispers in his ear his little song, if a piece of furniture creaks, if your voice or mine becomes a bit louder, he will wake up. He'll come here, and we will die."

"This is what I'm looking for," he murmured in a grim voice.

"I would die for you if I loved you. But I don't love you."

"So why do you risk death?"

"For mercy."

"Don't you feel anything else for me?"

"Friendship and pity."

"You women are wicked."

"Poor Fulvio!" she said very gently.

"I forbid you to feel pity for me. You must love me.

Do you understand? This is what I came to tell you."

"I can't love you."

"You must. I have the right to be loved. Ah, do you believe that a man's existence is nothing? Do you believe it's nothing to pass by a man and take away everything he has? Do you believe it's nothing to let him freeze and burn, giving him a fever that never stops? Do you believe that a woman can with impunity look sweetly, smile gently, speak softly, the way you look, smile and talk? Oh damn sweetness, damn sweetness!"

Despite the fact that he was very close to her and almost sensed the expression on Paola's face, he didn't see the tears that rose to her eyes.

"Because finally, I was a happy creature. I enjoyed my youth and the sun and the gaiety of my country and the joy of my friends! I had serene indifference, the greatest human happiness. I was selfish, but calm. I would let myself be loved; I didn't try to make people love me. Serene, serene like Jupiter!"

"May God restore your serenity," she whispered softly.

"God ... I don't pray to Him!"

"I do pray to Him, always, to give you peace."

"Oh, hypocritical woman! Don't make fun of the Lord, as you make fun of me. Listen. You must love me, necessarily. I love you too much not to be loved. It would be a huge injustice. There are no such injustices in the world. The world is balanced; everything is equalized. My flame is too strong, not to inflame you. You must love me. You'll leave your husband, your mother, your house, your servants, all that you have loved, all that you have adored, and you'll come with me. We will go far away. We will be very happy, very happy, you'll see. We will also be unhappy, I know; but it doesn't matter, such is life. Passion is stronger than us. I adore you, Paola, let's go away."

"You are crazy, my friend," she said, leaning her elbow on the parapet and looking at the sea below.

"No. Or if you like it, I'm crazy. This doesn't matter. The fact is I can't live without you. I need you. I want you. No one wants you like I do. Now nothing resists the magnetism of the will; it would liquefy a diamond, break the iron. You are a woman, you have human organs, you feel, you love, you hate, you will feel the magnetism of my soul that wants you. Your husband has you, but he doesn't want you: He is a beast. I hate him fiercely. I wanted to kill him tonight. I'll kill him tomorrow, if you don't leave with me. But you will come. You came to the terrace. You will leave with me. Let's go."

And he took her hand, resolutely, to take her away.

"No," she said.

"Come away with me."

"No."

"Why?"

"Because I don't love you."

"Oh Paola, Paola, don't talk like that," Fulvio cried out in a teary voice.

"How would you want me to talk?"

"Keep quiet, then. The sound of your voice, so sweet and so cold, makes me despair. Please be quiet, please."

She was quiet. Fulvio had thrown himself with his arms and his head on the parapet, suffocating his sobs. She had bowed her head on her chest, as if deep in thought. A carriage passed on the road to Posillipo, at a trot; a ringing sound of laughter came. Paola raised her head.

"Don't cry, Fulvio."

"I am not crying," he said desperately.

"Be strong."

"I'm very strong."

"Listen, listen to what your friend tells you. You will recover easily."

"No, never."

"You will recover. Are you honest?"

"I'm honest."

"Well, you will recover. Passion is a dishonest thing. I have a husband, you see. This seems like a vulgar answer, but it's honest, instead. When we are young girls, our mother tells us: You must love the man you marry. If you can't love him, at least you must respect him, you must be faithful and obedient, preserve for him your body and your soul, even at the cost of dying of sorrow. And these words not only our mothers tell us, but are exemplified in our daily life. This duty of honesty, this tradition of fidelity, this legacy of virtue, is transmitted to us in the blood, from mother to daughter. There is nothing sublime, you see: It is a duty, and we do it."

"And we die, Paola."

"We don't die. It is the passion, the blind passion, which insults the husband, the good husband who sleeps there, calm, confident, without suspicion. This is the great injustice. Because ultimately, the man who marries, even when he makes a marriage of interest or ambition, makes a serious sacrifice. He entrusts us his name and his heart. He gives us his faith and his freedom. He binds himself in an indissoluble bond. He begins to work for us and for our children, humbly and gloriously. We are his consolation and his glory: We represent for him the sweetest and safest of satisfactions. His day is spent in the desire to meet us again, to see us: His most cherished hours are in the house, in our arms. Oh, what a treasure of small and big sacrifices is the love of a husband! You ignore them. Passion ignores everything; it doesn't even know itself."

"Husbands betray their wives," he murmured, as if in a dream.

"They betray them, but they love them. Nothing is capable of defeating that deep bond, that intimate bond made of words and of tears, made of kisses and sighs. Nothing can break this bond that seeped deep in the heart and in senses. But here comes passion: It wants to defeat that sacred bond, wants to break that sacred bond. Who are you? A young man, a man, a random person in the multitude of men, far from me, a stranger to me. You follow your path: I, perhaps, cross yours. And immediately you love me. What have you done for me? Nothing. What can you do? Nothing. Or should I say, a lot. I have a name; you want to take it away from me. I have honor; you want to throw it away, like a rag. I have the esteem of my friends; I am asked to scorn it. I have the trust of my husband; I must betray it. I have the peace of my conscience; I must lose it forever. Why? Because you love me? Also the man who sleeps there, so quiet, loves me."

"It's not true."

"What do you know about it? Only we women know who loves us. Do you talk about rights? Oh poor sleeping man! Go, adore a woman to the point of marrying her. Give her the best part of your life. Put all your hope in her. Be to her a brother, a father, a husband, a lover, a friend, a counselor, a nurse. Suffer for her in body and soul! Here comes a stranger, a handsome, selfish man filled with his whims, a man who has done nothing, who offers your woman a life of dishonor. Here is one who, by violence, wants to take everything away from you! How can you speak of injustice? What are you doing here? Why do I even bother to listen to you, to defend myself, to give you explanations? I don't know who you are; I don't know you. Move away from my path. Go away."

"You don't love me, Paola, that's all."

"This is true, I don't love you."

But a fleeting light from her husband's room struck them both. A very brief flash, and then the shadow, again. Fulvio and Paola, looked at each other, understood. And quietly, softly, as if she were about to die, she said, "Blessed Madonna, I recommend to you my soul."

In a whisper, she prayed. Fulvio was silent, waiting. But no noise was heard, no light appeared, no one came. It had been a deception. They remained there, like this, for some time. He didn't dare interrupt that silence, say the last word. Everything seemed to have collapsed around him, in the black night, and he couldn't walk among the ruins. Yet raising his eyes, he sensed that her eyes were questioning him, eager for a conclusion.

"What should I do?" he asked glacially.

"You should go," she said with calm sweetness.

"Go where?"

"Where you want, but not here, in short."

"Very far?"

"Very far."

"Can I come back?"

"No."

"In a few years?"

"No, never."

"What will you do here?"

"Years will pass; then, I will die."

"Will I ever see you again, Paola?"

"Never again."

"It's death, this, for me."

She opened her arms, as if she had nothing to add. "Goodbye, then."

"Goodbye."

They didn't shake hands. He turned away, went back into the dark hall, walking like a sleepwalker. She listened carefully, following his steps through the house, and remained motionless, white. Then she saw him, from the terrace, walking alone, on the road to Posillipo, disappearing into the night, into the shadows, like a dead man. Only then Paola turned. A voice behind her said, "Paola, you love Fulvio."

She answered her husband, "Yes."

And two despairs looked at each other.

PAOLO SPADA

The man whose name you read above—a poetic and fateful name—was novel writer. Thirty years old, he was short, sturdy, stocky, with a short forehead, black and dark circled eyes, red cheeks, and thick, sensual lips. If for the figure of the novelist there is an established type that hysterical maidens and nervous women dream of—black, wavy hair, noble forehead, Arab pallor, pensive eyes, beautiful mustache, slim body—Paolo Spada certainly didn't match this imaginative ideal. He slept soundly for seven hours every night, had breakfast of eggs, steak, cheese, and wine, walked up and down the streets in the sun, lunched very well, danced, played the piano, went to the arms room, skated, and courted the ladies, as any excellent, strong, and courteous young man would do. As for his mood, he was almost always cheerful, with only brief interludes of melancholy. He loved good company, witty conversation, chamber music, and beautiful women with a Greek head. He had neither faiths nor doubts; he was indifferent. Every now and then he changed his girlfriend.

This good gentleman, so resembling any other gentleman, was also a novelist and short story writer. He had talent; not what is commonly called this in Italy and commonly possessed by every twenty-two-year old, the talent that makes people write poems free of any grammatical law, novellas without subject, and attempts at comedies without plot. He had a real, clean, bright, precise talent, something resembling steel. No morbidity in his intelligence, no sickly nervousness in his imagination; an austere and frank health, an almost muscular strength in substance and form. He admired all the writers whose genius, for mysterious causes— almost always physiological—becomes a disease. He was full of enthusiasm for the frightening, gloomy, bleeding, desolating visions coming out of brains drunk with love, brandy, or art. But his admiration was for the contrast, the opposite, the admiration that one holds towards an adversary, the salute in fencing, the just homage rendered to the enemy, because he was healthy in mind and body.

Thus his best quality was the keenness of observation. This cheerful and carefree young man, who breathed the air and the aromas from his quivering nostrils, whose only distraction was the gaiety and passed from one pleasure to the next, from one impression to another with youthful rapidity, had the sense or the intuition of observation. When he wrote, he seemed to remember scenes he had actually lived, or landscapes he saw. Nothing fantastic, nothing created by him, nothing that resembled an effort of imagination. His art was powerful in truth and expression. But there was no poetry in what he wrote.

***

Yet this Paolo Spada was the greatest dreamer I've ever met. He knew the secret pleasures of those solitary

161

hours spent laying in an armchair, contemplating the white ceiling on which a crown of roses is painted. He knew the tender movements of those slow walks around the house, in front of a painting, a portrait, near the fireplace, behind the balcony windows. He knew the secret of those excited walks, up and down the rooms, his head bent, his fists clenched in his pockets, seeing nothing, bumping into the furniture, saying a few words aloud. In those hours his door was closed; neither friend nor woman could enter. He was dreaming! And that dream was so vague, so little fluctuating, so alive, so real, so close that he almost could extend his hands to grab it. All the contours of a dream were defined, precise, with a neatness of lines almost too strong, filled with energy and prominence. The landscape revealed itself to him in its most intimate parts, in the most obscure recesses, in the vastest expanses; he saw it as in a painting, indeed better than in a painting, as it is in nature. He saw the scene of his novel unfold before his eyes, with the characters who were talking, acting, moving, hugging, killing, better than on the stage, as in real life. He throbbed, quivered, dared not move, dared not breathe; he was moved, feverish before his dream that was real life.

But where his dream reached its highest level of dream and reality was in the creation of his characters. He could see them; they appeared to him not as ghosts, but as living people. They looked at him, they talked to him, they lived with him, with the face he had given them, with that body, with those clothes, with that look, with that voice. Women especially. They came to see him in his dream hours. Young, brown-haired girls, with eyes full of light and goodness, with simple smiles;

blond and delicate women, moving gracefully, with red lips; dark-haired and beautiful women, with the eyes of a courtesan, provocative and voluptuous mouths; pale and mystical virgins, with bloodless faces and lean bodies; sinful women with made-up eyes and cheeks covered with white lead powder. They came to him in their satin, wool, or brocade dresses, covered in rags, in thin cotton, in lace, all blazing with beauty, smiling with goodness, transpiring melancholy, emanating the scent of Heaven or the perfume of guilt. They came to him, sat down, told him about their lives, wept, laughed, leaned their heads on his knees, hummed a little song, murmured sorrowful verses, played a song on the harp, stripped the petals of the flowers, and then, like Ophelia, they left, never to return. He knew them, he called them by their name, was familiar with their life. Some of them, the most strangely beautiful, the most mysteriously enchanting, the most cheerful or sad, hugged him and kissed him slightly on the forehead, because he loved her.

***

His first book of short stories, never seen before, because he didn't want to have them appear first in periodicals as is customary, caused a great sensation and raised many discussions. But no one could deny the power of the writer, the strong virility of his art, the purity and simplicity of his artistic means. As with all the first books, it was all a flourishing of ideas, a thick and intricate wood, full of bushes, a nourished and rich condensation of thoughts. As in all the first books, all lack of form was compensated by the enthusiasm that drags everything away by the heat that was transmitted to the reader. This robust and virginal book won the public's heart. Yet toward the end of each story, one noticed in the writer, and the reader felt it, a sense of malaise, like a painful feeling, like a latent thought that comes to distract from positive thoughts. Then the stories ended, as if truncated, without a conclusion, almost thrown away with disdain. One, in particular, about a little nun in love, ended so abruptly, so badly, that the hostile critics saw it as a serious flaw. The friendly critics replied that this was artistic disdain, and this was the impression of many others, so everyone calmed down, waiting for Paolo Spada's first novel.

Instead, he published a story of one hundred and eighty pages, interesting, subtle, written with the deep awareness of a novelist. Never had so much intensity and so much grace been seen before. It was a thoughtful, fresh work. Toward the penultimate chapter, all these qualities waned miserably, vanished. One could see the awkwardness of the beginner who doesn't know how to conclude the story. In the last chapter, the protagonist, who without a doubt should have died, somehow, without a reason, didn't die: she was fine and she married a random person. It was a mistake unworthy of an artist. After much praise for the beginning of the story, everyone strongly criticized the end.

After that, it always happened the same way in Paolo Spada's novels: His beautiful, good, bad, human female characters, sympathetic throughout the novel, at the end would become trivial and ridiculous. She who committed suicide, could not commit suicide well enough to die; the one who was destroyed by a serious consumption found a miraculous medicine that saved her, and married her doctor; the one who contracted meningitis, followed a strict regimen of quinine and healed; the one who, betrayed by her lover, was reduced to despair and wished to die, consoled herself without a reason in the world. Some of them, also, as in the first novels, suddenly disappeared, never to be heard of again. Thus, an entire emotional, psychological drama would end up in a marriage and a picnic. Thus, the whole work of art was spoiled, ruined by that illogical, absurd, bourgeois end. In that final stretch in which all the talent of the artist was lost, the book was lost. It was said that he was weak, that his talent had lucid intervals alternated by darkness. It was said that he could begin his books, but not finish them. The legend remained. And Paolo Spada's reputation as a novelist got lost among the endless mediocrities that afflict art.

***

I found out his secret. One evening, in an hour of friendly conversation, while I questioned him with my eyes, without speaking, he talked to me, enthusiastically, all about a new novel of his. I let him talk, admiring his vigorous face brightening up.

"And the protagonist, how does she end up?" I asked.

But I immediately regretted it, for I saw him go pale. "I don't know," he answered vaguely. "I don't know.

"Listen," he resumed after a painful silence, "listen to me, because I will tell you what I never told anyone. I'll explain to you the sorrow of my existence, what is the

165

ruin of my artist's ideal. Listen. The dream I write about is so real that it is like life itself. My heroes really exist around me. In me, with me, for me, my women exist. I evoke them, and they come. I created them, and they are my life, my creation, they belong to me, they love me. I love them without limits, without measure, with the most blind of passions. My love is not the Rosina that you know: It is Fulvia, of whom I am the creator and the lover. Fulvia, an ideal figure, is more a woman to me than Rosina. I write their story, with an emotion that drowns me, as if I were telling the life of the beings that I adore. I write, I write, happy, excited to let the public know their beauty and their love, exalted to the idea that these divine creatures will make other hearts tremble. Others like me will love them, these heavenly and loving girls, these passionate women. I feel the deepest pleasure given to the human spirit. But when their life declines, a subtle anguish takes me. I love them, and I can't see them decline. When they succumb to the illness that must kill them, I love them, and I let myself be won by melancholy; when they fall into the catastrophe in which they must perish, I am assailed by despair, because I love them. They should die, while I love them. I, the one who loves them, I should kill them. Briefly, or at length, I am supposed to describe their agony and then kill them. I can't. My heart is torn and I can't. It seems to me I am killing a living and healthy person by treachery. It seems to me I am drowning, in a dark corner, a woman without defense. It seems to me I am slaughtering a child at night. I can't kill them. Why should I kill a lover who is beautiful, who is good, who hasn't betrayed me? I can't. I horrify myself, and I can't. I wait, I think, I reflect, I torture myself. Art tells me:

Fulvia must die. And I cry out to her, sobbing: *I don't want her to die!* Art tells me: *Kill her.* And I consume myself in pain, crying: *I can't, because I love her.* I wait, in tormenting expectation. Nothing happens. So I save my dying creature in the least artistic way, in the most vulgar way. She lives, and I die. Isn't this ridiculous? But it's heartbreaking. These beloved figures whom I can't kill are killing everything in me—happiness and glory. I die giving them life."

AN INTERVENTION

I.

That day, Guido had the appearance of a happy man; serene forehead, laughing eyes and lips, a quick and loose walk. He was returning from a political banquet—in this case, the word *luncheon* is too vague— where, when the fruit was served, he had explained minutely to his voters his program, and the applause showered him. The chef's cooking, the champagne, and the candidate's program had produced a huge impression: The election was assured. In the evening, then, Guido would go to a dance where he would meet Baroness Stefania, a cruel woman, who, for a month, was seeking a dignified pretext to allow herself to be moved by him; perhaps, during a waltz by Metra or a poetic visit to the buffet, the pretext would present itself: Divine mercy is great. Taken care of his public and intimate affairs, Guido was coming back to sleep for an hour, like the great Napoleon on the eve of a battle.

But Giuseppe, an old and faithful servant, one of the only few left, Giuseppe remained in a respectful position in front of his master, on his face the desire to say something.

"Well?" asked Guido, who had noticed.

"I apologize, my master... I mean..."

"As long as you are quick."

"Master remembers what day is this?"

"No, Giuseppe, no."

"Today is your birthday..."

"Ah!" Guido said, a sudden furrow on his brow.

"Other times... in someone else's times... on this day, there were flowers everywhere..."

"They were, and there are no more!" Guido said with a slight sadness.

"There are, there are," said the old servant, showing a large bunch of flowers towering over a shelf.

"But...who...?" Guido asked, but looking at the servant's humble and smiling face, he understood right away.

"You, Joseph?"

"Master will forgive me..."

"No, there is no need to apologize. Thank you: You have pleased me with those flowers."

And the candidate to the constituency of Roccacannuccia and to the heart of Baroness Stefania was moved by the thought that on his birthday, only his servant had the kind idea of a gift of flowers. But it was a little emotion, because Guido was first of all a man of spirit. Now, those who belong to this honorable and restricted class of people, have the right to be moved sometimes, but as long as they do so briefly, without demonstrating it on the outside, and shortly after they are ready to smile about it.

"I'm going to sleep a little," said Guido. "You can wake me up at seven thirty."

"It would be better if Sir did not go to sleep."

"And why, wise Giuseppe?"

"Because this morning, while only Girolamo was in the house, a lady came. When he understood that the master had gone out, she said, 'Very well, as soon as he comes back, tell him that I will be back tonight at six o'clock, to wait for me at all costs, because I must speak to him of an urgent matter.' And she left."

"Good! And her name?"

"She didn't want to leave it."

"Uhm! Mysterious stuff, some little peregrine swallow. Did Girolamo tell you at least... what this was about?"

"No, but did say she was a young, tall, brunette woman dressed with great elegance."

"Better and better. My curiosity is tickled. So do you believe, Giuseppe, that because of this unknown person I shouldn't sleep?"

"It's six o'clock. If she's on time, the master won't

even have time to lie down on the armchair."

"All right, let's do this sacrifice to the unknown goddess. Giuseppe, give me my newspapers; I'll wait for her while reading. A brunette and tall: Right, Stefania has very blond hair; it will be a diversion."

Here the reader will raise her eyes from the page and think that Guido threatens to be a Don Giovanni. Not at all. I don't deny that at twenty, Guido had such a big heart to worship three women at a time, but a great passion had come to him once, a passion to which he had given all his heart, and then, with a wretched combination of events, happiness had collapsed like a castle of cards and the great passion was stifled and buried in the past. After two years spent in killing it, Guido had resumed his life as a young man, a little bit here, a little bit there, but they were fires of straw.

"Sir, sir," Joseph said, coming back into the room, very upset.

"Did she come?"

"She is in the living room."

"So you know her?"

"No, no…I don't know her," replied the servant, stammering.

But the master was already by the door of the living room, where he stopped for a moment to contemplate the unknown woman. She was standing by the table, browsing an album of photographs. She had turned her shoulders to the door, so that all you could see was a tall, pretty figure dressed in a rich dress of black cloth, full of lace.

"Madam," said Guido, advancing. She turned to him immediately: Guido felt like an electric shock, and to conceal the great wonder that appeared on his face, he bowed deeply.

"Am I bothering you?" she asked, sitting with great ease after answering his greeting.

"In no way; I'm at your disposal."

"Too bad that you are just being polite: I'm ready to take advantage of this."

"At my own risk and danger, then," replied Guido, smiling. "Please talk."

The lady, named Emma, caressed the soft hair of her muff a little; it looked as if she, confident of his ideas, was seeking an effective way of expressing them. Guido was distracted, looking at her. It was really she, always beautiful, always fascinating as the first day he had seen her; indeed, now she seemed to him complete, perfect. Her profile, always pure, was now more marked, firmer; her pale brown complexion had colored to a light pink rose; her eyes, once only lively, had assumed a deeper expression; that woman had lived and suffered.

"Have you ever played a part in a comedy?" she finally asked.

"Oh, I always do!"

"Very well, I see I have asked a useless question. So

tomorrow you will play a part again; but I warn you that you'll have to play a serious part, and that success will be difficult to achieve."

"Everything depends on actors and audience."

"You will have me as a fellow actress."

"I know your expertise."

"In pretending?"

"In acting. Will it be a moralistic drama, a *proverb*?"

"Yes, but without the moral of the last two verses. The morality is all in the purpose of this representation: It is what you might call a good deed."

"It comes from you," said Guido, with a veil of irony.

"What is that supposed to mean?"

"That you are merciful; and I still don't understand..."

"In a moment. And tell me... are you in touch with my father?"

"All time; but it must be two weeks since he last wrote me."

"I, instead, received a letter yesterday. He writes that he is well and that tomorrow he will arrive in Milan on the ten twenty train."

This time Guido didn't think he had to hide his

surprise. "Tomorrow?"

"Correct, tomorrow."

"Your father, the man who never goes anywhere?"

"He's going to Naples and he wants to do a short detour to see..."

"His daughter..."

"And his son, he says."

"So?"

"So we are in a bit of a mess," Emma said, stretching her foot over a velvety stool.

"You call this *a bit* of a mess?"

"I'm not used to make a big fuss. Yet we have to find a solution."

"I don't see any."

"And you call yourself a politician, a man of resources? What good is it for you to have learned the art of subtle subterfuges, delicate transactions, of the loyal and...very diplomatic phrases?"

"If you keep talking like this, I'll find it even more difficult to find a solution."

"Bah! I found it."

"I should have known."

"You are courteous even in your intentions."

"I would like to be such in everything, for you."

"We'll see. So, I was saying that there is a way. Here it is: Cost whatever it costs, I don't want my father to know the truth."

"The sad truth."

"An unnecessary adjective. My father would suffer very much for this, and I would have a tremendous remorse for his suffering: The parents must not suffer for the sins of the children. So far, thanks to my solicitude and yours, thanks to the distance, thanks to the fact that he doesn't know anyone in Milan, he was spared this pain. But tomorrow, all this beautiful building of pitiful lies could crash down, and God knows what the consequences would be. This must be prevented absolutely; you will help me in this work. He will find us tomorrow as he has left us; not a word, not a gesture, will reveal to him the true state of things. This is what we have to do."

All this was said in a calm and serious voice, and Guido had listened to her seriously. Yet he didn't reply immediately; he was thinking.

Emma grew impatient. "It's a comedy, as you can understand," she went on. "A comedy for charity. It won't cost you so much."

"As far as I'm concerned, I'm ready. But aren't you afraid of some misunderstanding?"

"Which one?"

"The servants..."

"Tomorrow you will use the new servant I hired this morning. And let me speak to Giuseppe."

"Very well. And if a friend should arrive inopportunely?"

"Tomorrow you won't receive anyone."

"I suppose we'll go and pick up your father at the train station, and we'll tale him back here. But the people who will see us together, what will they say?"

"People will not see us; we will go in a coupé, quickly."

"Your father will spend here a day; however good and naive, do you think he will not notice that he is in a bachelor's home?"

"This evening I have brought my work table, my books, and my music. It will be our stage."

"Yet…"

"Is there something changed in the rooms?"

"Nothing has changed," said Guido in a serious voice. "The room is intact, exactly as you left it."

"Are you being sentimental?"

"You're wrong. I am respectful."

"Thank you; do you have other objections?"

"None. It remains to see if we'll be able to deceive the good Mr. Giorgianni."

"Playing the affectionate newlyweds? We will remember the old times—the silly attentions of the first year of marriage," Emma said sarcastically.

"I had forgotten them," her husband answered promptly.

They looked at each other's face, exchanging looks like duelists evaluating the opponent.

"But maybe I'm selfish, demanding to kidnap you for a whole day. Do you have other commitments tomorrow?"

"No, none; if I had any, I would cancel them."

"Thank you again. For this evening, you are absolutely free; I don't need company."

"What do you mean?"

"Of course I'm staying here tonight. I'll wait for my things to arrive, as I told you, and in the meantime I'll arrange them, and then I'll disrupt them, so that they seem to have always been here. But I don't want to give you more trouble: Go out, come back when you like; until ten tomorrow you are a free man."

"In fact, I am supposed to go to a dance. Yet, if you'd like, I'll stay."

"And why? We would need to have a conversation, and there is nothing left to say between us.

"Oh, you're too right. So if you don't mind, I am going to dress."

Emma bowed, and Guido left the room like a man without any worries, a free spirit. But inside he was in turmoil: In fact, this event was wonderful to him, and as he thought about it, he fantasized about it, so that he was deplorably distracted at the dance. Baroness Stefania threw him furious glances that he had the impertinence of not seeing; indeed, taking advantage of a quadrille that kept occupied the whole room, he left without saying goodbye to anyone.

Back at home, he found himself in a transformed, unusual, new environment: The big salon, closed up for so long, had been aired; in the bedrooms all lights were lit, the closets were wide open, in the air was a subtle smell of violet. In the sitting room, the piano was open and the music sheets on the stand; fresh flowers were in the vases, the position of the furniture was different, and Emma, dressed in a dressing gown, was on her tiptoes to grab a statuette from an étagère.

Was that a dream? Emma at home, waiting for him...that is, the three years of her absence canceled, canceled that painful day of separation... how foolish.

"Good evening," said Guido, and passed by her.

"Good evening," she said, without turning.

II.

I have to confess, that despite the strangeness of the warnings, despite the doubts about tomorrow, in that house, that night there was no insomnia, nor tears on the pillows. Emma was persuaded that the little comedy to be performed would not change anything in their future, and Guido believed the same; they knew each other too well and knew that nothing, nothing could bring them together any more. Emma, entering her old room, thought to be in a hotel, and Guido, in his room, fell asleep after three pages of Herbert Spencer (I don't mean to slander the philosopher, but my hero was sleepy).

It was true; nothing could bring them together any more. To marry, they had committed all sorts of strange things: Guido had chased Emma from Florence to Naples, had spent nights under her windows; Emma would write him a letter of eight sheets each day, and would spend all night on the balcony. Her father, a bit willing, a bit forced, ended up allowing the marriage, as all the dads of this world do. Deep inside, he was a very good person and he had hesitated because he was sorry to be separated from his daughter. Yet, afraid of seeing her getting sick, he said yes. The two newlyweds, very happy, worshiped each other for three years in a row. I didn't say that they didn't have fights, or jealousies, especially on Emma's side. She had an extreme temperament, proud, fierce, unable to love or hate with moderation; Guido, instead, opposed her with that hint of coldness, with the ironic smile of a weak character. Sometimes they clashed badly, but peace was ever more beautiful.

One day, I don't know how, Guido met with an old flame; they saw each other again, they remembered, there was a note, a secret meeting. Guido let himself be dragged there more by weakness than by passion. More than anything, he was ashamed of his student-like behavior. How did Emma come to discover this? Was it an imprudent servant, a zealous friend, a lost letter?

Nobody knew, but there was certainly a clear proof of his betrayal, for all the blind and burning love she felt for her husband turned into a cold contempt. She couldn't find an excuse for him, she felt hurt to death in her affection and in her pride of a happy woman. She called her husband, and with a marvelous calm, without ever letting her voice tremble, told him that they would split without screaming, without scenes. He was stunned by surprise; he wanted to react, smile, take it as a joke, minimize his guilt, but his wife answered him with such fervent and stern words that he had to remain silent. It seemed ridiculous to him to continue to justify himself. He accepted all the conditions that she imposed to him and let her go; he judged her a superb and loveless woman. He tried to distract himself, as I have said, in business, politics, lovemaking. He assumed a frank countenance, he showed himself careless and skeptical; but only in the company of his conscience, he felt that his life was shattered and ruined.

He saw his wife two or three times, from afar; they exchanged greetings like two people who barely knew each other. The one never sought the other; after all, she led a very lonely life, never attending theaters and parties, while he threw himself into noisy amusements. They agreed only on one point: They would keep writing to her father as if nothing had happened; that is to say, formal news. For example, Guido would write: "Emma is fine, I think she wrote to you; she sends you her love, sends hugs to her aunt." And Emma would write: "Guido is fine, he is very busy, he can't go with me to the baths." So Mr. Giorgianni's happiness was attached to a silk thread.

Seeing each other again after that last and cruel day, husband and wife were very upset. In order to come to her husband's house, to overcome her hesitations, to assume that gay and ironic attitude, Emma had to tame her pride. *For my father, for my father!* She kept repeating, to find courage; but what had really helped her was Guido's gentle coldness. Theirs had been a courteous dialogue, obsequious, without allusions to the past or the future, except for some slight quip. There had been no drama, no recriminations; they had behaved like wise, positive people. And tomorrow?

Tomorrow would be the same: a bit of fiction, a bit of spirit, be calm, never betray themselves, conceal their anxiety under their smile, say a bunch of officious lies, and take dad back to the station, to wave big goodbyes and split: each one on his way. A reconciliation? Not even the idea. Guido would never have said the first word; Emma would never forgive him.

Each one had a peaceful mind.

III.

They had just finished dining, Mr. Giorgianni smiled, happy and blessed, and the two actors tried to smile as well. But all that seemed easy the night before became very difficult at the time of performing it. Since that morning, on the arrival of her father who had joined them in a hug, they were obliged to call themselves by name, to use those affectionate courtesies that are typical of couples still in love, and because of a word, an intonation voice, a fleeting memory of the past, Guido would turn pale, Emma blushed, and a visible embarrassment reigned among them.

Despite the fact that they were willing to do anything, that they had thought of the misunderstandings that might arise, that they were trying to forget their personalities, reality would impose itself at every moment and brought confusion in their minds: It was useless, they could not suppress their conscience. Add to this the fear that for a slight imprudence they could lose all their praiseworthy efforts, and the vague but persistent idea that this scene thus interpreted could create something new or unexpected between them.

On the stairs, while Mr. Giorgianni preceded her, Emma glanced at her husband in desperation, and the meaning of that look was "How will we keep this up till tonight?"

And he, in reply, an expressive look: "Let's help each other, that fate will help us."

And so on. But at home, the dangers doubled. Mr. Giorgianni seemed to find pleasure in finding risky topics, in asking naive questions that were troubling those who had to answer the poor and good father who loved his children so much!

"Yes," he said, after laying his cup down. "I'm so happy for this half-day spent with you. See, Emma, the letters are a good thing for those who are far away, but I prefer visits, even for a few hours. You, my daughter, are fine, but you've become more beautiful, more elegant. Isn't it true, Guido?"

"That's what I always say to her," Guido said,

smiling.

"And he also writes it to me! Oh! For this, my daughter, I can assure you that Guido in his letters does nothing but talk about you; one would say you've bewitched him. What a model husband!"

"Indeed," Emma agreed in a low voice. There was a moment of silence after the wife's answer. Guido had bent his head and seemed to count the tablecloth flowers.

But that day, Dad was talkative: "Aunt Elisabetta sends her greetings. She's always a bit of a grumbler, but she really loves you both. You, Emma, were her favorite, and now she only talks about you...."

"She's a good aunt."

"The best. Do you know what she was telling me a little while before my departure? 'I'd be happier if my dear Emma had a pretty little child...'"

But here Mr. Giorgianni, in spite of his joviality, realized that he had committed an imprudence; he saw that Emma's face went all cloudy, and he saw that his son-in-law twisted his mustache nervously.

"Also Rosalia, your cousin," he said, then to change the topic, "also Rosalia is fine. But she has had a lot of sufferings."

"Oh! And why? Didn't she marry her beloved Piero?" asked the daughter, with a bit of irony.

"Yes, yes, she married him, and they loved each

other much. I don't know how, I don't know why, Piero had a whim, for a Neapolitan lady..."

"You call it a whim, Daddy?"

"Yes, it was a fleeting whim; don't be pessimistic. But Rosalia suffered a lot because of it, weeping, scenes..."

"Bah!"

"I tell you, Rosalia ran back to her mother."

"Good for her!"

"Very bad, I say. A wife never abandons her husband. Finally, it was I, with my eloquence, persuaded her to forgive him, to erase that debt..."

"You, Father?"

"Yes, and I am delighted with my intervention. Because being uncompromising about these things always ends up ruining our life: Men sometimes make mistakes against their will..."

"Convenient moral," Emma said firmly.

"It was your mother's moral, my daughter."

"What? Mother, too, thought better to forgive?" Guido asked with great interest.

"Sure, sure. That woman was full of mercy and indulgence: She was good, good, good. He who loves well, she used to say, forgives much."

They all remained silent and pensive; and Mr. Giorgianni, to break that silence, exclaimed, "So, my children, are you going to show me this apartment, this silk and velvet nest? I only could give it a quick glance."

"Let's go," said Guido. "We will start from the salon."

"Magnificent, magnificent," Mr. Giorgianni said when they arrived there. "This is perfect for big receptions. Do you organize parties?"

"We used to."

"I understand, now business and politics prevent you from seeing too many people, but the salon is beautiful. And this living room, what exquisite taste! Were you, Emma, the one to choose?"

"No, it was Guido."

"I congratulate him. He probably thought that you would have liked to spend time mostly in this room; here are your worshipers to court you, no doubt, eh, naughty girl? Aren't you jealous, Guido?"

"I? I know my wife."

"What about you, Emma?"

"I know Guido too much."

The two responses were quick. Mr. Giorgianni was satisfied. "This bedroom is a wonder," he resumed, "and its colors form a sweet harmony. All this white and gray is soothing to the eye."

He moved about the room, as if looking for some missing object. Finally he called his daughter, who was standing on the threshold. "Emma?"

"Father?"

"Where's Mom's portrait? I don't see it."

She became confused, unable to answer.

"We were in Brianza," said Guido, "and not all our belongings are back yet."

"That portrait should have come first. No matter; Emma can't have forgotten her mother. What a woman, what a woman, my dear Guido! Too bad that you didn't meet her! When she wanted to go, poor woman, she promised that I would have sacrificed everything for Emma's happiness, and so you could say that she, too, contributed to your marriage. When Emma came to tell me, 'Daddy, without Guido I'll always be unhappy,' I thought of my dear dead wife and I decided. You were made for each other: You had been in love with each other for a year, Emma was becoming pale and sad; you, Guido, were going out of your mind. Youth, youth! Do you remember, my daughter, of that dance at the English consul's that you attended with Guido?"

"I remember," she replied mechanically.

"Seeing your serene and happy faces, the looks you exchanged, everyone understood that you were engaged, and they called me a lucky father! Yes, very lucky, I add; you loved each other even too much."

"Never too much," Guido said.

"It's true. Let's hope this is always so, won't you, Emma?"

"Let's hope, Daddy."

"And this closed room, what is it?"

It was Guido's room; in turn he found himself confused, and Emma came to his rescue. "It's the guest room, Daddy."

"Ah! Good, good. The room I would have occupied if I could have spent the night with you. It's unfortunate, but I have to leave soon."

"It's very unfortunate," said his son in-law.

"It doesn't matter: I'll console myself looking at it, instead of inhabiting it."

"But..."

"I understand, it will be messy, it doesn't matter!"

Guido bravely opened the door; he could no longer hesitate. "Not bad, not bad. This, too, is pretty like the rest of the house. Oh! Look here! Who put here the portrait of my little girl? Certainly it was a kind thought of Guido; thank you, my dear. But I can't stay. How sorry I am!"

They sat in the living room. Husband and wife were very distracted, and if Mr. Giorgianni had been a bit more keen, he would have suspected that something strange was going on between them. But fortunately, the good dad was not very smart.

"Too bad." He said, "It's a pity for this beautiful house!"

"Why is it a pity?"

"Because you'll have to leave it soon. If they elect you as a deputy, as it is almost certain to happen, it will be more convenient for you to stay in Rome for at least six months out of the year, and I don't think you'll want to abandon Emma alone in Milan. You will need two houses, it will be inconvenient; yet, there is also something that makes me feel good. If you come to live in Rome, I will be able to visit you at least once a month: from Naples to Rome, the journey is short and convenient, while from Naples to Milan, it takes forever! So we will see each other often."

IV.

When the two heroes got into the carriage, after having accompanied their father to the train station, when they were finally alone, they gave a great sigh of relief. It was finally over; their life would resume their regular course. They were not talking. Emma watched the raindrops on the coupé glasses; Guido did not give a sign of life. They were strangers again.

At one point, Guido, moving, hit his wife's arm. "Excuse me," he said.

"It's nothing."

Strangers, that's true. Yet, in that silence, they both thought back of the facts of the day; they remembered the most minute impressions, and felt them again.

"Should we turn here, to go to your house? Guido asked at some point along the way.

"No, I'll come to your house: I have to put together my things, because my maid won't know how to do it. I'll leave later."

"Very well."

At home, she went straight into her room. Guido threw himself on an armchair in the living room and pretended to read a newspaper. In fact, he heard her come and go with her slow steps, he also saw her pass by him two or three times. "Are you tired?" he asked. "I could help you."

"No, thanks; I am almost done."

In fact, shortly after, she also came to sit down, looking very tired; the day had exhausted her. She looked around as if to find something she had forgotten. "It's raining less, I think," she told Guido, who had abandoned his newspaper.

"It is still raining."

"Is the carriage not ready yet?"

"I don't know; let me go check."

The carriage would be ready in ten minutes.

"Do you want me to accompany you?"

"There's no need, thank you."

Did it seem like a century, or an instant, those ten minutes? Perhaps both.

When the servant came in to say that everything was in order, Emma got up resolutely and went to put on her hat in front of the mirror; it took some time to tie the ribbons, because her fingers were slightly trembling. Then, slowly she put on her gloves, buttoned them, adjusted some folds in her gown, and proceeded towards Guido to say goodbye. He stood up, very pale.

"Goodbye," she said.

Guido didn't answer: She turned her back and crossed the living room, straight, proud, without staggering, with a steady and equal pace; yet she sensed that her husband was following her. At the door, she raised her hand to the handle and met the quicker hand of her husband.

"You forget to forgive me, Emma," he said with a voice in which pain and passion were fighting.

She turned suddenly and threw her arms around his neck, suffocated by the love reawakening, powerful, between them.

"You'll never go away again, dear?"

"No, no; send someone to take my mom's portrait, Guido."

THE PUBLISHER

You think this is another short story, don't you? Well, you are half-right. We've included another short story here from our collection, *The Demon Deer and Other Animal Stories* by the Nobel Prize-winning author Grazia Deledda. We hope you enjoy it. But first, a word from our sponsor, which is us!

Kazabo Publishing is a new idea in the literary world. Our motto is, "Every Book a Best Seller . . . Guaranteed!" And we mean it. Our mission is to find best-selling books from around the world that, for whatever reason, have not been published in English. Matilde Serao's short stories are very popular in France and Italy but very few have been published in English. Why? We don't know. But we think you will agree that they should have been. And now they are.

We have found there are also many contemporary writers who are very popular in their own countries but who have not made it into English. We think this is a real shame so we are working to bring those books and those authors to you.

When you visit Kazabo.com (our website!), we hope you will always discover something new, either a book from a favorite author you didn't know existed or a completely new author with a fresh perspective from a country you admire. We promise you that everything you see with the Kazabo name – even authors you have never heard of – will be a best-seller; maybe in Italy, maybe in Japan, maybe in 1902, but a best seller. We hope you enjoy reading these literary gems as much as we enjoy finding them and bringing them to you.

But enough about us. Here is an excerpt from our Grazia Deledda collection entitled "The Bull."

Thanks for reading!

The Kazabo Team

Kazabo.com

THE BULL

By Grazia Deledda

The appointment was at six o'clock, but by five the woman, greedy and impatient as women are, was ready to go out. She went out, then she went back in to wear her red silk knit jacket, but she left it very open on her breast, bronzed with a seaside sun tan.

The air had suddenly cooled down, and she was very attentive to her health and her body. When she arrived in the chilly street, she regretted not having taken her scarf to cover her head. But she thought she was already late. She was afraid to meet someone who would make her waste time, and she pressed on. The wind passed over the large plane trees, and it did not bother her until the avenue narrowed to become a small country road that looked like an embankment, high between the vineyards that descend to the sea. Up there the wind was playing at leisure with the young poplars and with the oats growing along the ruts of the road. Suddenly it seemed to notice the woman and assaulted her, ruffled her hair, which began to irritate her and make her think. She knew very well where she was going and why, but, suddenly, as if the fresh air and the mischievous wind cleared her mind, she felt almost offended by all the precautions taken, more by her man than herself. They were to meet in a distant place, to go on different roads, even though they had gone together and alone a hundred times, with the freedom that the outdoors give to the holidaymakers. Those same roads, without worrying about anyone, happily arrive at that same point and even beyond, and go no less happily back.

But then they didn't stop, while now there was the tacit understanding both of them were to do so.

But perhaps at that hour, he too, was walking up the sandy road that, from the sea, passes between the vineyards and crosses with the one she was traveling, accompanied by the harsh wind. This hope made her step up, and the wind then annoyed her even more, as if thinking she had escaped from it. It swelled her thin clothes to make her look like an iridescent bubble of soap, and above all it ruffled her hairdo, showing what was fake and exposing the silver threads, hidden like moon beams among night clouds.

She arrived, almost tired, at the crossroads. She looked right and left. To the left, the sea was shimmering, and to the right was another grassy, tree-lined street, quiet between vineyards and lonely fields. Nobody. The sound of the wind in the trees answered only to the murmur of the sea and her heartbeat.

She turned to the right, crossing to the sunny side of the road because she was almost cold. The wind now left her in peace, again busy with the thick foliage of the robinia trees sheltering the road, and she walked slowly, a bit humiliated that the man was not here to meet her.

She was the first to arrive at the appointment.

In her heart, she felt that her state of mind didn't correspond with that blind passion that ought to have pushed her forward and made her happy with her impatience, her humility, and the small difficulties she had to face, and this was what made her feel most humiliated.

Every now and then she turned back. She sat on the parapet of the bridge over the ditch and waited. Women on bikes were passing by fast, touching the grass like swallows. Carts passed by, led by women who whipped the horses and encouraged them with a virile voice. One of them smoked a pipe. It seemed like a country inhabited by women who thought of anything but love.

The man was not to be seen. What if he was already in the assigned place? She jumped down, resumed her way, arrived a quarter of an hour early at the place of the meeting. The place was solitary—picturesque, but solitary. It was a poplar grove at the end of a meadow, where the vineyards ended and the land began with its meager pastures and the horizon marked by the sad wrinkles of the rice fields.

Between the columns of the poplars were horses and cows in the pasture, and the grass was so fine that it invited one to touch it.

But the man was not to be seen. She went back to the road, and stopped at the corner between this and the meadow. The sun illuminated her, making her jacket look ablaze.

And suddenly she realized with horror that a large, heavy bull, rosy as if covered by human flesh, was approaching her with his head lowered, without looking at her, dazzled by the color of her clothes.

As long as she stayed still, he remained quiet. He seemed to be driven by curiosity more than anything else. But it was an instant: she started to run, and the beast mooed powerfully, running behind her.

Other moos answered, hoarse, deep. She felt like she was chased by an entire herd. She also saw red, and instead of running down the street, where she could have escaped behind some gate, she ran towards the grove. Perhaps she instinctively hoped that the man would help her. She didn't know. She didn't even have the strength to shout. She only felt the beast behind her, with his bellowing like a sea monster, and she had the impression of swimming, of losing her strength, of drowning.

Here she is, in the grove; she stumbles on a branch, falls, gets up again, quick, and resumes the race. But the beast has gained ground, and now she really feels his heavy gallop and fiery breath close by, and her hips and bowels tremble as if they had been already wounded by the monster's horns.

So she began to scream, but who could hear her?

"Oh my God, my God!"

Perhaps God heard her. She ran to the end of a poplar grove and passed near a lumberjack's cabin, almost without seeing it. The little door opened quickly, mercifully, fearfully; she got in, frantic, and she was able to close it. Just in time. The beast was there, behind the little door that stood heroically against the crashing, but was trembling all over. Wood and woman were one single trembling thing, clinging to each other to create a bit of resistance; but the woman felt that she didn't have long if God didn't help her.

She believed in God.

"My God, my God, I know I have forgotten everything. And I came here to sin, to betray, only driven by boredom and by this miserable flesh..."

Outside, the bull pushed and bellowed. The little door, as if disappointed by the woman's crude confession, was falling, tired. The fragile lock gave out.

The woman began to scream, asking for help, but she felt she was sinking, like a drowned person.

Outside, a shot burst, and the bullet arrived whistling, sure of itself. The beast fell heavily as if his legs had been cut off; and the woman, too, let herself fall, fainting.

The man had to compensate the herdsman who arrived at a run shortly thereafter. However, his friend didn't go walking with him anymore.

THE END (Really!)